## Rose raised her voice.

'I warn you, I shall do everything I can to stop you upsetting my postnatal patients and antagonising perfectly reasonable staff.'

As she got up from her chair, Leigh finally lost his patience with her. 'Rose, for heaven's sake! Damn it all, Phil is a paediatric registrar!'

'Big deal. And I'm a woman,' she returned.

'And may I ask if you've ever breast-fed a baby, Dr Gillis?'

'Not yet, Dr McDowie. Have *you*?

**Dear Reader**

Marion Lennox gives us a quite spectacular setting in THE LAST EDEN, and two fascinating people in Ellie and Leeton for you to enjoy. In HANDFUL OF DREAMS, Lucy is shocked to inherit a school, and in A BORDER PRACTICE Dr Lyall Balfour is a mystery for physiotherapist Lindy to solve. Dr Rose Gillis has the uncomfortable job of bossing a man who is senior to her in rank in A SONG FOR DR ROSE — Margaret Holt has created a super character in Leigh. Four very different stories, but all enthralling! See you next month.

*The Editor*

**Margaret Holt** trained as a nurse and midwife in Surrey, and has practised midwifery for thirty-five years. She moved to Manchester when she married, and has two graduate daughters. Now widowed, she enjoys writing, reading, gardening and supporting her church.

Margaret believes strongly in smooth and close co-operation between the obstetrician and the midwife for safe care of mothers and their babies.

**Recent titles by the same author:**

A MIDWIFE'S CHOICE
A PLACE OF REFUGE

# A SONG FOR
# DR ROSE

BY

MARGARET HOLT

MILLS & BOON LIMITED
ETON HOUSE 18–24 PARADISE ROAD
RICHMOND SURREY TW9 1SR

To my neighbour
Anthony Lewis Fussell
who listened.

First published in Great Britain 1993
by Mills & Boon Limited

© Margaret Holt 1993

Australian copyright 1993
Philippine copyright 1993
This edition 1993

ISBN 0 263 78135 6

Set in 10 on 12 pt Linotron Times
03-9306-51201

Typeset in Great Britain by Centracet, Cambridge
Made and printed in Great Britain

# CHAPTER ONE

THE whole of the north-west was enjoying a heat wave, and the Manchester suburb of Beltonshaw lay shimmering in a windless, dusty haze. All the windows of Beltonshaw General Hospital were open to their fullest extent, and the scent of roses drifted up to the ante-natal and delivery unit. Maternity patients were sitting out on the secluded little lawn beside the rear entrance to the department, and waved to Dr Rose Gillis as she hurried to the doctors' mess for a hastily snatched lunch, her white coat unbuttoned over a light, sleeveless summer dress. She was house officer for obstetrics and gynaecology, an attractive young woman of twenty-six whose creamy skin was accentuated by her raven-black hair, now swept back into a neat coil.

'Over here, Rose!' called surgical registrar Dr Paul Sykes as she carried her salad and coffee on a tray from the serving-hatch; she smiled and joined him at his table. They made a handsome couple, and colleagues daily expected an official engagement announcement, though closer friends knew that they had decided to wait for at least two more years before tying themselves down to marriage. Meanwhile there was the caravan at Nethersedge in the Lake District, and Rose knew that Paul would expect her to escape with him from Beltonshaw's stifling heat next weekend when they would both be off call. The caravan had been a good investment, though Rose was uneasy about what her mother would say if she knew of their ongoing

5

relationship: Mrs Gillis assumed that Rose's weekends in the Lakes were shared with a mixed group of colleagues.

The insistent peep-peep-peep of the electronic bleep in Rose's top pocket could not be ignored. She got up from the table, walked briskly to the nearest wall telephone, and asked the switchboard to put her through to wherever she was summoned. It could be the delivery unit, the antenatal or postnatal wards, Gynaecology, Theatre, Clinics or Accident and Emergency. Or it could be Mr Horsfield, the consultant obstetrician and Gynaecologist, with whom she had requested an appointment that afternoon, to ask for an extension of her housemanship. It had been her own decision, uninfluenced by Paul Sykes; Rose was her own woman, in control of her life and career.

'Dr Gillis? Oh, can you come up to Antenatal straight away? Mrs Mowbray's having another epileptic fit!' There was no mistaking the urgency in the midwife's voice.

Rose replaced the receiver and made a wry grimace in Paul's direction before hurrying off along the hospital's main lower corridor and up the stairs to the antenatal ward, which shared a floor with the delivery unit. She reflected that she and Paul had made the right decision—marriage was not a good idea for hospital doctors on call.

A nursing auxiliary directed her to the patient's TV lounge, where she found Sister Tanya Dickenson and Staff Midwife Laurie Moffatt kneeling on each side of an unconscious Mrs Mowbray, whose rigidity and jerking movements of the hands and head showed that she was having an epileptic fit of the *grand mal* type, with loss of consciousness and bladder control.

Rose's heart sank, though she remained outwardly calm. Mrs Jane Mowbray was a lifelong epileptic, normally well controlled by daily medication, but the complex hormonal changes of pregnancy had completely disrupted her equilibrium, and fits were occurring almost daily. She had been brought into hospital for supervision, and was now thirty-four weeks into her first pregnancy, which meant that there were another six weeks to go before her baby was due.

'When did this one start, Sister?' asked Rose, kneeling beside the two midwives.

'About three minutes ago, as she was watching the news on TV with some other antenatals,' replied Tanya Dickenson, the efficient newly appointed sister in charge of the antenatal ward. 'We've sent them out, of course — some of them are very upset. I've managed to get a metal spatula between her teeth, and the airway's unobstructed.'

'Can we get her head turned over on to one side?' ventured Rose, placing her fingers firmly behind Jane's lower jaws in an effort to push her chin forward and so obtain a better air entry.

'Be careful, Dr Gillis!' cried Laurie Moffatt as the patient ground her teeth convulsively. Her face and lips were turning unpleasantly blue, but Rose involuntarily withdrew her hand, and felt a moment of helpless panic.

Then a firm, hurrying step was heard in the corridor, and a tall, rather untidy figure breezed into the lounge, his longish hair curling over a crumpled white collar. Rose breathed a silent prayer of relief at the sight of Dr Leigh McDowie, one of the medical registrars. They had met on previous occasions when the physicians had been asked to see maternity patients with medical problems such as diabetes.

'Hey! Buck up, girls, don't just kneel here saying your prayers,' he chided, expertly manoeuvering the padded metal spatula between Jane's clenched teeth. 'Got any tongue forceps handy? Off you go, Laurie, and fetch me a pair—and ask somebody to lug an oxygen cylinder up here!'

Within thirty seconds the convulsion began to pass off, and Jane Mowbray's body relaxed. Her eyelids fluttered, and she drew a deep breath voluntarily. When the oxygen arrived, Dr McDowie gave her a few whiffs of it through a light plastic face-mask, and her skin became healthily pink. He had no need to use the sharply curved forceps that prevented the tongue from blocking the throat.

'Hi, Jane! Don't worry, love, everything's all right. We'll get you on to the trolley and take you back to your bed for a nice long sleep,' Dr McDowie told the woman gently. Looking up at the midwives, he added, 'Always keep the oxygen at hand, girls, wherever she goes—to the bathroom, the lounge or kissing her husband behind the door—she needs to have it handy. The baby needs it even more,' he muttered.

The auxiliary brought in the stretcher trolley, and he lifted Jane Mowbray off the floor, heaving himself up and placing her carefully on it. She did not speak, but smiled in a bemused way like a person suddenly roused from a deep sleep. Sister Dickenson immediately put up the cot sides, clicking them into position, and Rose followed the trolley along the corridor to the ward, where Jane was gently transferred to her bed.

'Somebody must sit with her for a bit,' ordered Leigh McDowie. 'She'll need to see a familiar face when she wakes up. Give her a stat dose of phenytoin, a hundred milligrams, and the daily dosage had better be upped to four hundred milligrams—we can't go higher than that because of Junior—and carry on with the phenobarbitone at night. Heigh-ho! Cue for a cup of tea all round, I'd say—right, Tanya?'

Tanya smiled agreement and sent the auxiliary to the kitchen to prepare a tray, while a student midwife was detailed to sit beside Jane Mowbray's curtained bed.

Sitting at the office desk with the two midwives, Leigh McDowie stirred his tea and made himself quite at home.

'You know, ladies, the old man's going to have to get that poor girl delivered sooner rather than later,' he commented.

'Yes, that's just what we've been saying,' nodded Tanya, a tall, slim-built girl with pale ash-blonde hair that was almost silver in some lights. Her cool light blue eyes appraised this deceptively easygoing man whose thick dark hair was so unprofessionally long. His quizzical brown eyes returned her look boldly, while also taking in the more ample attractions of Laurie Moffatt, another blonde, giggly and good-humoured.

Rose stood a little apart from them, beside the specially constructed trolley that held the patients' case-notes in strong cardboard wallets. She was studying Jane Mowbray's records, and was trying to subdue a flicker of annoyance with this doctor, even though she had been so thankful for his timely arrival and his unflustered management of the situation. She disliked hearing Mr Horsfield referred to as 'the old man', and also felt that Dr McDowie's airy request for tea had been cheeky. Had he no responsibilities in the medical wards? And that ridiculously long hair for a hospital registrar in his thirties!

As if he had heard her thoughts, Leigh McDowie turned round in his chair and smiled cheerfully at her.

'Don't you agree too, Rosie? The poor little Mowbray nipper isn't enjoying having his mum flaking out all the time — cuts down his oxygen supply drastically. No fun for either of them, is it?'

'No doubt Mr Horsfield will consider an early delivery, but thirty-four weeks is a bit soon, and the baby's not very big, according to the scan report,' replied Rose carefully, not looking up from the case-notes.

'Maybe not, but he — or she — won't get much bigger if he's got to put up with this sort of caper every other day,' he argued. 'And we can't just keep on pumping more dope into the unlucky woman, because he won't like that either. Little chap'll be stoned out of his mind!'

'I absolutely agree with you, Leigh,' said Tanya firmly. 'Besides, it's so embarrassing for Jane, and upsets the other antenatal mums. Some people are so irrationally terrified by epileptic fits!'

Rose stiffened. 'I'm sure Mr Horsfield will take all factors into consideration,' she said coldly.

'Do I detect a note out of tune, Rose, my love?' enquired Leigh, pouring himself another cup of tea. 'I mean no disrespect to our revered consultant — in fact I'll lay you a pound to a penny that he'll do a Caesarean on her before thirty-six weeks.'

Rose flushed slightly, and made no reply.

'Oh, Rose, when you blush it's like sunrise over snow,' he said admiringly. 'And how did you come by those gorgeous deep blue eyes combined with black hair? It's pretty unusual — I mean it's pretty and unusual — unless you've got Irish blood somewhere back in your ancestry?'

'My mother's people were from County Clare,' said Rose briefly, noticing the shrugs and grimaces being exchanged by the midwives. It was obvious that Tanya did not share Leigh's interest in this subject.

'Ah, I knew it! I recognised the Celtic soul in you,' he said, and heaved a melodramatic sigh. 'Sykes is a lucky swine, getting in front of me at that Hallowe'en party—you should have seen her, Tanya, she was absolutely stunning as the Wicked Queen of Narnia, but I was on call that night and so all my hopes were blighted. Why do women always go for surgeons rather than physicians?'

By now Rose was thoroughly irritated by Leigh McDowie's nonsensical talk, and when he broke into a Scottish love-song, she felt no obligation to stay and listen, though the midwives smiled in surprise at hearing the perfect pitch of his clear, true tenor.

'O, my Luve's like a red red rose
That's newly sprung in June——'

Without a word Rose marched off down the corridor and into the ward to check on Jane Mowbray, now sleeping peacefully and naturally, as epileptic patients usually did following a fit.

Leigh's song drifted after her on the warm air of the summer afternoon, and the words were strangely insistent, lingering in her head, in spite of her resentment of him.

'O, my Luve's like the melodie
That's sweetly play'd in tune——'

The mothers-to-be in the antenatal ward looked at each other in delighted admiration.

'Is it on somebody's radio?' asked Mrs Lambert, who had a low-lying placenta.

'No, it's that nice long-haired doctor—ain't he

smashing!' sighed Trish, the toxaemic teenager whose boyfriend could only sing raucous rugby songs after an evening out with the lads.


'Ah, Rose, my dear, how are you? Sit down, sit down,' invited Mr Horsfield, who always meticulously addressed her as Dr Gillis while on duty and in the presence of others. To be called Rose in this fatherly way was oddly comforting, and she wondered if he sensed her nervousness as he waved her towards a comfortable armchair beside the open window of his office, instead of talking to her across his desk. He seated himself a few feet away from her, and they looked out at the roofs of the Manchester suburb now blazing in the heat; the trees in Beltonshaw Park were deepening into the darker, dustier green of July after their first freshness.

'It's good of you to see me, sir,' began Rose, conscious of his sharp though kindly eyes peering over the top of his gold-rimmed half-moons. Even on a hot day he wore an immaculately tailored grey suit and his fellowship tie.

'Not at all, my dear. I think we should have a little talk anyway,' he responded. 'Your work for the past six months as junior house officer has been splendid, quite splendid. I've been gratified to see how much you've developed your skills, and of course your next step should be to find a registrarship for a couple of years. I haven't in fact got a vacancy until next year, but in any case you should go somewhere else now, to widen your experience. See how they do things down in London or up in Edinburgh!' He beamed at her. 'I'll be delighted to give you an excellent reference, you know that.'

'Thank you, sir, I appreciate that, but I have a particular reason for wanting to stay in Beltonshaw just now,' said Rose hesitantly.

The consultant frowned.

'Oh, you *women*!' he said testily. 'People accuse me of male chauvinism, but it's not my fault that so few women reach the top of our profession. You throw your own careers away! Time enough to settle yourself down in one place when you've got a husband and a family to look after! I'm a firm believer that motherhood should take precedence over all other careers while there are children to be brought up, as you know——'

He paused and they exchanged a smile of understanding. Everybody knew his views about the prime importance of a mother's duties.

'But you're young, intelligent and *free*, my dear girl!' he went on. 'You've got plenty of opportunity yet to advance yourself before you get tied down with a family. Why on earth should you stagnate in Beltonshaw just because that registrar in general surgery—what's his name, Sykes—has decided to dig himself in and study for his fellowship, no doubt with an eye to stepping into Mr Mason's shoes?'

Rose squirmed with embarrassment at his bluntness and accuracy.

'I have to advise you to move on, Rose,' he continued. 'There have been housemen who've needed an extension of time, but not you. Of course, you're welcome to stay on if you really wish it, working all the hours God made for a pittance, but you should move on to new pastures while you still have time.'

Rose fidgeted in her chair, furious with herself for blushing crimson. 'It isn't only because of—of Dr

Sykes, sir,' she said awkwardly. 'Quite apart from the
fact that the experience here as a house officer is of
enormous value, there's another consideration.'

He waited. 'Yes?'

'It's my mother, sir. I'm not too happy about her.
She's a widow and lives in Beltonshaw, so I can keep
an eye on her, which is convenient.'

'Go on,' he prompted. 'Why aren't you happy about
her?'

'I suspect it's your department, sir,' she replied. 'I've
at last persuaded her to see our GP. She's had a slight
prolapse for years, with the usual symptoms and a
tiresome discharge ── '

'God save us, woman! And you call yourself a
doctor!' exploded Mr Horsfield with untypical vehemence. 'You've let your own mother suffer for years
when all you had to do was bring her to my gynae
clinic! I find it hard to believe, Rose.'

Rose closed her eyes momentarily and put a hand up
to her forehead.

'It's not that simple, Mr Horsfield,' she protested.
'You don't know her. She comes from an old-fashioned
backwater in Ireland, and has been on her own for so
long. I'm her only child, and we've never talked about
intimate matters. She can be quite stubborn, and has
never really looked on me as a doctor, though I know
she was pleased when I got my degree. I've only
managed to persuade her to see Dr Tait since I
discovered by chance that she's been losing a little
blood, and I think she might have a cervical erosion, in
which case ── '

'How old is your mother?' demanded the consultant
sternly.

'Fifty-five this year, sir.'

'And she's passed the menopause?'

'I—I presume so, sir. She's never mentioned it.'

'Now listen to me, Rose. Mrs Gillis is to come and see me tomorrow morning at nine—no, make it a quarter to nine, before my clinic begins.'

'It's very good of you, sir, but——'

'Bring your mother to me for an examination at eight forty-five tomorrow. Is that quite clear?'

'Yes, sir. Thank you.'

And then the penny dropped. Post-menopausal bleeding: Mr Horsfield automatically suspected cancer. Rose's eyes filled with helpless, shameful tears.

'Whatever must you think of me?' she faltered.

'Oh, my dear girl, I understand—perhaps better than you realise,' he said with a sigh of regret for some private memory. 'We don't always want to face facts when they apply to ourselves and our families, even though we may be very quick to make pronouncements on strangers. The very fact that you've told me about your mother shows that it was there in your mind, just below the surface. I'll see her tomorrow, and we'll get to the root of the trouble, whatever it is.'

'I'm very grateful to you, Mr Horsfield,' she said simply.

'Glad to be of help, my dear. Now, you say you want to continue as SHO on Obs and Gynae for a further six months. Very well—with two weeks' leave, that will take you through to the middle of January. Difficult to picture that in all this heat! I'm glad to keep you, Rose, and I'll get a contract drawn up for you with the Beltonshaw Health Authority.'

He smiled, and not for the first time Rose thought what a perfect old dear he was.

'There's just one thing that I should point out to

you, Rose,' he went on, and she could almost imagine she saw a gleam of mischief behind the half-moons. 'You'll be senior SHO this time, and your junior will be Dr Leigh McDowie, who's senior to you in all other respects. A rather unusual situation, you'll agree!'

'*Dr McDowie!*' exclaimed Rose in astonishment. 'But how—I mean, he's a medical registrar!'

'*Was* a medical registrar,' corrected Mr Horsfield. 'He plans to go into general practice eventually, and feels he needs to recap on obs and gynae—so he's taking demotion for six months as a junior SHO. Very good man in his field, of course, a highly individual approach, and I wish he'd get his hair cut, but that's by the way. He could learn a lot from you, Rose! I must admit that it will be an asset to have an up-to-date physician on the team, to advise on our diabetics, asthmatics, heart murmurs, epileptics—oh, yes, that reminds me, I'm going to section our Mrs Mowbray on Monday.'

'Oh, really, sir?' said Rose with interest.

'Yes. It's one of those difficult decisions, a choice of two evils. Would the baby stand a better chance inside its mother or in the special care baby unit? In her case I've come down on the side of the latter. Do you agree, Rose?'

His eyes twinkled, and Rose smiled in spite of herself, remembering Leigh McDowie's comments.

'Yes, sir, I most certainly do,' she told him, getting up from the armchair and shaking the hand he held out to her.

'Good luck, my dear. And I'll see you tomorrow morning in Outpatients, with Mrs Gillis.'

\*    \*    \*

Slipping into the doctors' mess for a quick cup of tea before going home for an evening and night off, Rose found the place deserted.

'Haven't you heard, Dr Gillis? There's been a big accident — a pile-up on the M63,' said the girl at the serving-hatch. 'All the doctors have gone down to A and E to lend a hand with the casualties.'

'Oh, how dreadful!' cried Rose, who had been closeted in the gynae theatre for the past two hours, assisting Mr Rowan, the obs and gynae registrar, with an afternoon list of minor operations — three D and Cs, a cone biopsy and removal of a Bartholin's cyst.

'Yes, it was a real mess, so I've heard,' the girl went on with a certain relish. 'Caroline Trench and her boyfriend were on their way home from the Granada studios after filming all day, and they were run into by one of them great articulated lorries!'

'Caroline Trench!' repeated Rose. The actress's name had become a household word since her success in a TV series.

'The driver was killed outright, and Caroline and her chap were badly knocked about — it's been on Radio Manchester,' continued the girl as Rose listened in horror. 'And a whole lot of cars ran into the wreckage before they realised what had happened, so lots of people were hurt, and they've been brought in here. It's *heaving* with police and ambulances down in A and E, Dr Gillis!'

'My God,' muttered Rose. 'I'll have to go down there to see if I can do anything.'

'Ooh, Dr Gillis, rather you than me!' shivered the girl. 'Here, have a cup of tea before you go, to keep your strength up.'

Rose had been looking forward to a quiet evening at

home, and a frank but tactful talk with her mother, but she knew that the accident victims would prey on her mind if she did not offer her services. Swallowing half a cup of hot tea, she ran a comb through the black tendrils that had escaped from the coil at the back of her head, and set off back to the main hospital building.

Never before had Rose seen anything like the scene in Accident and Emergency at half-past five on that summer afternoon. All the examination-rooms were full, and extra stretcher trolleys had been brought along to accommodate the dozen casualties who were being assessed for priority of treatment, cleaned and given tetanus vaccine. X-ray staff had been recalled, and nurses transferred from wards; the hospital chaplain, Father Naylor, hurried from one to another with pity in his eyes as cries of pain and sobs of anguish filled the air; and over all hung a sickly, pervasive smell compounded of blood, dirt, vomit, perspiration and an extra element that Rose never forgot—it seemed to be the very odour of pain and fear. She braced herself.

'Where's Dr Sykes?' she asked a hurrying staff nurse.

'Over there in Examination Three,' replied the girl, thrusting an intravenous giving-set and a plastic litre bag of glucose and saline into Rose's hands. 'Here, take this to him, will you? I've got a family of three in Room One to clean up!'

Rose grabbed the IV set and quietly entered the examination-room, closing the door behind her. A deathly pale woman lay on the couch, her red hair bloodstained, her clothes torn and disarranged. Rose recognised Caroline Trench, aged thirty-something. She was apparently unconscious, and made no movement as Paul Sykes lifted each eyelid in turn, and shone an opthalmoscope into the pupils.

'Ah, hello, Rose,' he murmured. 'Good, you've brought some IV fluid. Sister has deserted me while she gives out tetanus jabs, so could you give me a hand with putting up a drip?'

Rose took the tourniquet she always carried out of her pocket and fixed it firmly round Caroline Trench's arm to make the veins prominent. A faint moan of protest came from the white lips, and Paul leaned eagerly towards her.

'Caroline—Caroline, can you hear me?' he asked softly, his lips close to her ear.

The patient frowned, gave another sighing moan and then very slowly nodded. Paul gently took hold of her hand.

'Don't worry, Caroline,' he told her quietly. 'We'll look after you, and you'll be fine after a while. Just trust us, Caroline, dear.'

He looked up at Rose with a smile of relief.

'She's regaining consciousness,' he whispered. 'I don't think there's any serious head injury—just a fractured tib and fib, and multiple lacerations. She'll be OK, thank God.'

'And—her companion?' breathed Rose.

He shook his head. 'D—O—A,' he mouthed silently.

Rose shuddered. Dead on arrival. She experienced a hollow sinking of her heart at the thought of the suddenness with which this dreadful calamity had struck the busy motorway. In just a few brief moments of violence, death had claimed two victims and lives had been irrevocably changed.

The staff nurse Rose had seen before suddenly put her head round the door of Room Three without ceremony.

'Dr Gillis, can you come and help out in Room One?'

Paul Sykes frowned angrily.

'Sssh, Nurse! We're trying to put up a drip on a very shocked patient,' he hissed.

'So's Dr McDowie, only he's got three to see to, and he's all on his own,' snapped the unrepentant staff nurse. 'There's a married couple who've been thrown right across the motorway, and a young girl who's —'

'All right, Nurse, I'll come straight away,' said Rose. 'You're into the vein now, Paul, so you can just run in the fluid. I'd better see what's happening.'

As soon as Rose entered Room One, the choking smell of burned and soiled clothing rose sickeningly to her nose and throat. Dr McDowie and the staff nurse were cutting off the trousers of a man aged about forty who lay groaning on one of the two couches, his wife sitting beside him. Her face was streaked with tears and dirt, and a rough dressing above her right eye was held in place with a hastily applied bandage. On the other couch a girl of about eighteen writhed from side to side, gasping and moaning at intervals. The oppressive heat and foul air made Rose's stomach heave, but she summoned up all her self-discipline and professionalism as she prepared for action, and as if in answer to a wordless prayer, she received a certain sense of calm in the midst of havoc; she was a doctor, and this was where she was needed.

'Right, Dr McDowie, what's to be done?' she asked.

He looked up and smiled as easily as if greeting her in the bar of the residency.

'Hi, Rose, you're as welcome as a win on the pools. Meet Mr and Mrs Bradshaw — Alfred and Grace. They've been chucked around on the M63 quite a bit, and Alfred has lost a fair amount of red stuff. Dear little Nurse Kitty here is giving out morphine like free Biros, and I want to get a drip going as soon as we've cleaned Alf up a bit.'

'And the young lady?' enquired Rose, going over to the restless girl on the other couch.

'Ah, yes, that's Peggy Bradshaw, who was travelling in the car with them — their daughter.'

'Not daughter, Doctor — Peggy is my husband's niece,' cut in Mrs Bradshaw.

'Correction — niece. If you could deal with young Peggy, it would be a godsend, Rose. She's either got internal injuries or a bad attack of the vapours, and I'm inclined to go for the latter diagnosis.'

'Peggy's obviously in pain,' retorted Rose, picking up the girl's hand and feeling for her pulse.

'If you mean she's throwing herself around as if she's been stung by a hornet, you'll find that her pulse and blood-pressure are normal, and she won't answer a single question. Could you calm her down for us, Rose? It would do us all a favour, because quite frankly I haven't got time for an in-depth counselling session right now.'

Rose sensed his irritation and lack of patience with the girl as he re-applied himself to Alfred Bradshaw's needs.

'Kitty, me darlin', hand me that Venflo cannula — keep still, Alf — there we are! We'll get a couple of pints of blood cross-matched for you, meanwhile here's a nice drop of Beltonshaw Special Brew running in — OK?'

Leigh adjusted the flow of intravenous glucose and saline solution, and Rose turned her back on the group to give all her attention to the girl.

'Easy now, Peggy—ssh! Stop making that noise and tell me where the pain is,' she said in a voice both kind and firm. The only response was an agonised grimace and an even louder groan as Peggy clutched at the lower part of her tummy.

Rose stood looking down at her, and in a flash realised what was happening. She began to remove the girl's tights and knickers, and the sight of the fresh blood did not surprise her.

'Did you know you were pregnant, Peggy?' she whispered in the girl's ear.

'I—I wasn't sure. I haven't told anybody,' gasped Peggy. 'Uncle and Auntie don't know—oh, help me! Help, *help!*'

'Keep calm, Peggy, and hold tightly on to my hand. Be brave now, it'll all be over in a minute,' whispered Rose. Raising her voice, she said, 'Nurse, I shall need some syntometrine soon—could you fetch an ampoule from the fridge?'

'Good God, whatever for?' asked Leigh McDowie. 'This is a multiple road traffic accident, Rosie, not the delivery unit!'

Rose spoke very quietly and levelly to the staff nurse.

'Go and get me an ampoule of syntometrine at once, Nurse—*at once!*'

The nurse glanced doubtfully at Leigh McDowie, and with Peggy's next strong, expulsive pain, a foetus of about the size of a closed fist appeared, still intact in its bag of membranes and with the tiny placenta attached. Rose judged it to be of about ten to twelve weeks' gestation. She reached for a plastic receiving-dish from a shelf, and quickly placed the products of conception in it, covering it with a paper towel and depositing it under the wash-basin.

'Oh, *heck*!' exclaimed McDowie. 'Oh, thanks a million, Rose — I shall have to resign and get a job as a plasterer's mate —'

Rose turned blazing blue eyes upon him, and mouthed the two words, 'Shut up,' with a meaningful glance towards Peggy's uncle and aunt.

'Have I — have I lost it?' whispered Peggy, white-faced and trembling.

'Yes, dear. Don't worry — ssh,' whispered Rose back to her, snatching the ampoule from the wide-eyed staff nurse without a word, and drawing up the injection into a two-millilitre syringe. 'Just a little jab to stop you bleeding,' she murmured.

'Is Peggy all right?' asked Grace Bradshaw. 'I've been so taken up with my Alf that I haven't paid much attention to his niece. She's hoping to start at Manchester University in September, poor girl. Do you think she'll have recovered from her injuries by then, Doctor?'

'Yes, Mrs Bradshaw, she'll be fine,' Rose reassured her. 'Don't worry. We'll admit her to a hospital bed just for tonight. Female Surgical must be full up, but there'll be some beds in Gynae, I'm sure.'

She caught Leigh McDowie's raised eyebrows, and ignored his look. If the girl decided to tell her aunt the truth later, that would be up to her, decided Rose; she did not consider it her duty or her business.

Once the intravenous drip was up, Mr Bradshaw's general condition improved noticeably, and he was admitted to Male Surgical for observation. Leigh McDowie had made a provisional diagnosis of ruptured spleen and internal haemorrhage. Mrs Bradshaw was told that she could go home by ambulance.

'Let's just check a few details with you, Grace,' said the nurse. 'I mean your address and next of kin——'

'Yes, what about your kids?' asked Leigh. 'Can I get a message through to them for you?'

A look of unresolved bitterness came over Grace Bradshaw's streaked face.

'We haven't got any children, Doctor, after thirteen years of trying,' she told him. 'We had all the tests done, and we've given up hoping now.'

'Sorry, love,' said Leigh, while Rose seethed inwardly. This man had been getting on her nerves all day, and this final hurtful tactlessness was the last straw.

'My dear, you obviously have a very loving marriage, and your husband's life has been spared,' she said gently. 'I congratulate you.'

'Thank you, Doctor,' answered the woman with tears in her eyes. 'Thank you all for what you've done for us, and God bless you.'

By seven o'clock Accident and Emergency had been cleared, and the staff were drinking tea from plastic cups dispensed by the Women's Royal Voluntary Service, whose local members had come in specially because of the major incident, to re-open the refreshment bar and help organise trolleys and wheelchairs.

Sipping her tea, Rose wondered whether Grace Bradshaw would ever know that her husband's niece had succeeded in conceiving a child she did not want, while they had failed to achieve conception after so long; Peggy's aborted child was the third life to be claimed by the M63 accident which had taken Caroline Trench's driver and fellow passenger.

'*Rose*! There you are!' How can I ever thank you

enough for turning up when you did? You were an angel straight from heaven!'

Leigh McDowie, his white coat filthy and blood-spattered, and his hair sticking to his forehead in thick damp strands, stood towering in front of her.

She looked up with ice in her dark blue eyes. 'I think the less said about that the better, Dr McDowie.'

His shoulders slumped apologetically. 'Yes, I know how you must feel, Rosie, and I'm never going to forget missing that spontaneous abortion — what a gaffe!' he confessed. 'I'm so grateful that you came in and took over at that point, and I just want to acknowledge the fact, that's all.'

Rose stood and faced her junior SHO, tight-lipped and unsmiling.

'I can forgive you for missing a fairly obvious miscarriage, Dr McDowie, given the circumstances at the time, but what I object to is your general attitude — your total indifference and impatience towards that poor girl, your tactlessness with Grace Bradshaw who's obviously hung up over her childlessness — and your infuriating compulsion to crack feeble jokes on every occasion, no matter how inappropriate. I don't think it's going to be appreciated in such a sensitive field as obstetrics and gynaecology.'

'Oh. I see.' He flushed slightly as each clear word struck home. 'I'm very sorry to have so irritated you, Dr Gillis.'

'Not so much irritating as just plain boring, I'd say,' she rejoined, making the most of her advantage after a day of mounting resentment. 'Yes, to be honest, I find you boring.'

For a moment he stood open-mouthed and drop-jawed; then he recollected himself, and his mouth set in a very straight line.

'Good of you to let me know, Rose. Thank you. To be irritating is bad enough, and to be a poor practitioner is even worse. But to be boring — well, that's a very serious charge.'

He held out a hand to her. 'Look, Rose, we've got to work together for the next six months, right?'

She ignored his hand.

'Yes, Dr McDowie, and as long as you remember that we are doctors and not stand-up comedians, we should be able to survive it. Only I'm not much good at one-liners.'

And turning her back on him, she walked out of the department, where the unpleasant smell still lingered, mixed with detergent and disinfectant. Leigh stood and watched her go.

'Goodnight, Dr Gillis, but not goodbye,' he said under his breath. 'So I bore you, do I? You don't bore me. Quite the contrary.'

# CHAPTER TWO

PERSUADING Brigid Gillis to attend the gynae clinic was not easy.

'Heaven knows why ye want to subject your own mother to a man's interference!' she protested, her faded blue eyes full of reproach. 'Ye know me beliefs, Rose; I'm willin' to bear wid women's trouble if it's sent to me. Have ye iver heard me complainin', now?'

'No, Mother, and I only wish you *had*!' retorted Rose crossly, though she was now fully alerted to her mother's thinness, pallor and lack of energy. The transparent skin moved her to pity and a sense of urgency. How could she *not* have noticed earlier? Her heart ached as she contemplated the loneliness of her mother's life, teaching at a primary school and sacrificing everything to her only child—the piano lessons, the smart school uniform and additional expenses of the prestigious convent school from which Rose had emerged with good A-levels to go on to Manchester University and medical studies.

And yet there had been a strange reticence between them, and times when Rose had been conscious of an unspoken sorrow. She had learned not to ask questions about the early death of the father she could not remember, and the one blurred photograph of a young man in sailor's uniform left her oddly unmoved. How tragic that he had been drowned so soon after marrying and setting up home with Brigid in Beltonshaw, far from the Irish girl's native green hills. When Rose had asked why her mother had not returned home after being widowed, Brigid had replied that there were better prospects for her daughter in Manchester. How much she owed to the quietly devout woman, and how careless she had been in not seeing the insidious onset of illness. . .

'No more arguments, Mother! You'll find Mr Horsfield an excellent doctor and a perfect gentleman,' she concluded firmly. It cost her an effort to defy her mother, but Brigid had been left to bear her own burdens for long enough, and from now on Rose intended to share them.

At a quarter to nine promptly Mr Horsfield beckoned them into the examination-room, where Mrs Gillis's case-notes had been brought from Medical Records. A fractured clavicle following a fall from her bicycle years ago had been her only previous contact with Beltonshaw General. Rose had been born in Liverpool shortly before the move to Beltonshaw, so there were no maternity records; Rose thought how interesting it would have been to peruse the familiar blue pages, divided into Antenatal, Labour and Puerperium sections, if she had been born here.

The clinic sister remained discreetly outside the examination-room while Mr Horsfield took Brigid's medical history. She was not an easy patient to question; the enquiries about her bowels and waterworks embarrassed her, and she repeatedly insisted that she was 'fine for me age', though she gradually responded to the consultant's cool, professional manner, neither over-friendly nor too distant. At last he put aside his pen and said he would carry out a complete medical examination and the gloved 'internal' which she most dreaded.

When Rose stepped forward to help her mother undress, Brigid absolutely refused.

'I'll not have ye standin' here watchin' your own mother,' she muttered. 'Send in that decent-lookin' body in the blue dress and take yeself out, or I'll not remove a stitch!'

At least Mr Horsfield will realise some of the difficulties I've had with her, thought Rose wryly as she left the room and went to get a cup of coffee from the WRVS cafeteria.

'I didn't expect to see you down in clinic this morning, Dr Gillis! Shouldn't you be up in Maternity?'

The cheerful voice made Rose spin round to face Dr McDowie, who was smiling down at her. His clean white coat and shining, newly-washed hair curling over the collar was in complete contrast to the apparition of the evening before, and his friendly informality made her feel a little awkward about their sharp exchange then.

'I've had to bring my mother in to see Mr Horsfield,' she explained briefly as she sipped the coffee. He was immediately concerned.

'Oh, what a bother for you, Rose! He'll get her sorted out, though, won't he? You've brought her to the best gynae man in the north-west.'

His penetrating brown eyes searching hers with such real sympathy made her suddenly long to confide in him, to tell all her fears, doubts and regrets to this exasperating new colleague. She flushed slightly, and he seemed to be reading her thoughts as he tried to reassure her.

'Not the easiest of situations, is it, when a close relative has to see one of the firm? I had to bring my father up to Dr Stephens last year when the old boy developed what I thought was diabetes, but it wasn't. Frankly, I find that we're quite often wrong over diagnoses when somebody we love is concerned.'

His voice softened as the word *love* was spoken, and for a moment they were enveloped in a special shared intimacy of insight and understanding. Rose could only look up in frank gratitude for his forgiving spirit after her parting shot of last night.

'Thanks a lot, Leigh.' Impulsively she touched his hand, and immediately felt her cold fingers held firmly in a warm clasp.

'Chin up, Rose — and good luck to your ma!'

But when she returned to see Mr Horsfield's grave expression her knees went weak. What was she about to hear?

'Well now, Dr Gillis,' he began, 'I've just been telling your mother that she'll have to come into hospital as soon as possible. Tomorrow's Friday, and I want her in for the weekend, so that we can do a full blood count, group and cross-match a couple of pints to give pre-operatively.'

Rose went white and her blue eyes darkened with fear as he continued in a firm, matter-of-fact tone.

'On Monday we'll take her to Theatre and do a cervical biopsy, and wait for an immediate microscopy report. And then, my dear, I think it very likely that I'll proceed to do a total hysterectomy.'

Rose gasped and put out a hand to grasp the edge of the desk at which he sat.

'Sit down,' he ordered quietly. 'Steady, Dr Gillis.' He glanced briefly in her mother's direction, and raised his voice slightly.

'I've told your mother that I want her in by tomorrow morning, and that she'll feel much better after a weekend's rest and two pints of blood to get her in good shape before surgery. Take her home now and get things packed and ready, and I'll speak to Gynae Sister about a single room. We must provide the very best care for Dr Gillis's mother!'

He got up and shook hands with them both.

'You've got a good daughter there, Mrs Gillis, so be sensible and help her to help *you*. You're off this weekend, aren't you, Rose?'

Rose thanked him, pulled herself together and took her mother home. When she returned to the hospital, all her colleagues were anxious to make things easier for her. Mr Rowan waved her aside as he combined a houseman's jobs with his own responsibilities as senior registrar, and when Leigh McDowie came up to check on Mrs Mowbray's medication he also clerked in three antenatal admissions for Rose. Paul caught up with her in the doctors' mess at midday.

'I say, I'm sorry about your mother, but I'm glad something's being done straight away,' he sympathised. 'Er—I suppose we won't be going over to Nethersedge this weekend?' he added hesitantly.

'No, Paul, not with Mother in hospital and waiting for——' she faltered, biting her lip.

'All right, love, it's OK. What about dinner at the Old Barn on Saturday evening? It'll be nice to relax beside the river after the heat of the day.'

'Thank you, that sounds lovely.' She forced a smile. 'How's Caroline Trench?'

'Not too bad today, though I've had to be quite stroppy with reporters. And that photographer—what's his name, Maynard—wanted to take a picture of the poor girl in bed, complete with bandages, plaster and drip,' he told her grimly. 'She's got terrific guts and said she wouldn't object, but I wasn't having it. "On your bike, mate," I said in no uncertain terms!'

'Has she been told about her — her friend who was in the car?' Rose enquired cautiously.

'Not yet.' He frowned. 'She's been told he's "very poorly". She'll have to be informed soon, though. Mr Mason's on holiday, so I shall have to do it. Not a job I'm looking forward to.'

Rose shivered at the thought of breaking the news of death. She could not bring herself to face her worst fears, that she had been too late to save her mother. On leaving the mess, she went straight to the hospital chapel to pray for strength and courage, both for her mother and herself, in the coming ordeal — and for Caroline and all patients in need of hope and comfort.

At ten o'clock on Friday morning Brigid Gillis was installed in a single room in the gynaecological ward, and met Sister Kelly, a genial, buxom woman of Irish descent who had a broad Mancunian accent.

'Aye, we all love Dr Gillis, a right sweet lass and champion house-doctor! We're that pleased because she's staying on another six months,' she beamed, and when Brigid saw Rose in her white coat with a stethoscope round her neck and pocket bleep beside her identity badge, she at last began to realise the affection and respect her daughter commanded. A drowsy contentment came over her as she lay back on her pillows, and she closed her eyes. . .and opened them to find a tall, well-built doctor with unusually long hair standing beside her bed.

'Mrs Gillis?' His friendly smile was so infectious that Brigid smiled back in a way she seldom did at new faces.

'That's me, I'm Brigid Gillis, Doctor.'

'Good. May I call you Brigid?' he asked, sitting down on the bed. 'How are you settling in? Got everything you need?'

His dark eyes roved over the objects on her bedside locker, which included her alarm clock and a prayer-book.

'Sure, everybody's very good to me here. It must be because of Rose—that's me daughter, she's a lady doctor, Doctor.'

They both chuckled at the repetition, and he nodded knowingly.

'She certainly *is*, Brigid. And she can be a little terror if things aren't to her liking. Oh, yes, I've been on the receiving end of her sharp tongue, I can tell you—nearly broke my heart!' He heaved a melodramatic sigh.

'Good heavens, Doctor, are ye tellin' me that a slip of a girl like Rose actually told ye off—a *man*?' asked Brigid, horrified.

'Ah, yes, she's one of these liberated career women, and absolutly *ruthless*,' he went on, grinning from ear to ear.

'Oh, get away wid ye, Doctor, ye're havin' me on!' she scolded, her pale face alight with amusement. 'And who might yeself be, comin' in here and talkin' about me daughter?'

'Take pity on me, Brigid. Me name's Leigh McDowie, and I've got to take orders from that cruel woman for the next six months,' he groaned in mock despair. 'Please, I've come to ask you to put in a good word for me—will you, Brigid, me darlin'?'

'Sure, I will that, Doctor—and yet I've a feelin' that ye can stand up for yeself very well,' Brigid added slyly.

He held out his hand; she took it, and from that moment they became friends. After he had left the room, she found on the locker a miniature bottle of Irish whiskey liqueur and a get-well card with a picture of a cottage garden beside a stream.

When Rose arrived an hour later with Paul, bringing an African violet in a pot and a tin of mixed fruit-drops, they were surprised to hear her praise of 'that lovely doctor wid his hair on his shoulders and a look in his eye' — and Rose was grateful for anything that brought a smile to her mother's face.

Rose almost wished that she were on duty that week-end. She could not sleep in the quiet house, and when she got up early on Saturday the bright sunshine showed up a dimness and dustiness that had settled over the furnishings in recent weeks. She determined to set to work on an orgy of house-cleaning, washing down paintwork, polishing surfaces and rubbing at the windows until they sparkled. Down came curtains to be washed at the nearby launderette, and out went carpets to be beaten as they hung on the clothes-line. To see the little house looking bright and spotless again gave her some satisfaction, and she felt a flicker of hope when she visited her mother that afternoon. Although a blood transfusion was in progress, Brigid looked calm and relaxed.

'It's much better in here than I was expectin', Rose,' she confided frankly. 'Ye should have told me that it's like one o' those four-star hotels where grand folks go for their holidays!'

Rose smiled affectionately, looking down at the worn, blue-veined hands clasped together over the prayer-book.

'It certainly seems to be doing you good, Mother,' she remarked, recalling how the tired blue eyes had flashed so defiantly two days earlier.

Brigid put her head on one side and glanced enquiringly at the young woman doctor.

'Tell me, Rose, are ye really so hard on that lovely doctor wid the long hair?'

Rose looked a little embarrassed.

'Oh, you mean Dr McDowie. Don't take too much notice of him, Mother, he's full of nonsense — though I believe he's very good in his own field.'

'Never mind about fields, Rose, I can tell he likes you!'

Rose shrugged. 'That's good, because we're going to be working together. It's nice that he visited you. Paul sends you his love too, and he's taking me out to dinner this evening. I'll come and see you again tomorrow, Mother, and is there anything else you'd like me to bring in? More lemon squash — or tissues? Any book or magazine you'd like me to —— Mother?'

Rose's voice trailed off as she saw that Brigid had fallen into a light doze. Rising to her feet, she very gently kissed the smooth forehead before tiptoeing out of the room. She did not stop to speak to Sister Kelly for fear of betraying her emotion.

The arrangement for dinner with Paul had been made, and, although she would have preferred a light supper at home and an early night, Rose duly showered and changed into a light blue chambray dress with a woven belt, and applied just enough make-up to hide her pallor and the shadows under her eyes. She swept her raven's-wing hair back into a ponytail caught in a blue ruched satin ring, stepped into sandals and greeted

Paul with a smile when he came to call for her at seven-thirty.

During the drive through the green and golden Cheshire countryside, he politely enquired about her mother, and she longed to open her heart fully to him; but instead she put on a bright face and said that her mother was looking more rested.

'Very glad to hear that, love,' he said. 'I wish I could say the same for Caroline Trench. The poor girl's in an awful state now that I've told her about her boyfriend's death. To tell you the truth, Rose, I almost called off this evening's dinner, but I know how much you need to get away from things for a few hours' relaxation — and to be honest, so do I.'

'We've both had a difficult time this week,' remarked Rose, and wondered whether to suggest that they cancelled their arrangement; she decided it would be too ungracious, and might lead to an emotional scene that she would find hard to cope with.

'It's all rather complicated, actually,' he went on. 'He — Caroline's friend — he was — well, still married to somebody else, and there'll be the wife and kids to consider. At least Caroline won't be fit to attend the funeral, so there shouldn't be too much embarrassment over that, but inevitably the newspaper johnnies are bound to make a big thing of it, and the poor girl's terribly upset.'

'She's young, she'll get over it,' said Rose with a certain briskness. 'I'm sorry for her, but without knowing the full circumstances, I can't help pitying the wife and children. It's a double loss to them, isn't it?'

'As you say, we can't comment on the set-up,' agreed Paul, staring at the road ahead. 'Anyway, Caroline will be in Female Surgical for at least a month, and with a leg in plaster it'll be a long time before she can get back to her work. You should see the flowers she's been sent! They must think a lot of her at the studios.'

Rose closed her eyes for a moment and saw her mother's calm face asleep against the bank of pillows, the African violet and the prayer-book beside her.

Business was brisk at the Old Barn that evening, and a waiter steered them to the corner table that Paul had booked. As Rose ordered a halibut steak, she suddenly heard a girl's peal of delighted laughter from a lively group seated a few tables away, and, turning, she recognised several staff from the maternity department. Tanya Dickenson was smiling up at Leigh McDowie, and Laurie Moffatt, whose laughter Rose had heard, was seated opposite them. Further along the table were the two medical students from the University Hospital who were currently doing their six weeks' obstetric practice at Beltonshaw General. The five of them seemed to be indulging in a great deal of teasing and banter, and Rose lowered her head, not wanting to be seen by them.

'McDowie seems to have started off well with the two best-looking midwives,' observed Paul. 'Is he escorting them *both*, or is one of them with the student double act?'

'They've probably all just come out as a party,' said Rose, and wondered why she should care. What on earth did it matter to her whether Dr McDowie was with Tanya or Laurie or both? Yet she stole another look in his direction, and this time he was saying something to Laurie which was sending her into further fits of giggles.

'You've got to hand it to the man, he knows how to enjoy himself,' commented Paul.

'Good for him,' replied Rose with a slight shrug.

A roar of welcome went up from the group as a latecomer joined them. It was Roger Maynard, the freelance photographer who had taken a series of pictures of a celebrity and her baby who had been born in the maternity department earlier that year, and who had been sent packing from Caroline Trench's bedside by Paul Sykes.

'Hi! Sorry I'm late — have you started without me?' he greeted them.

'Roger, old son! What kept you? Wouldn't she let you go?' demanded Leigh as the photographer took a seat beside Laurie Moffatt and kissed her apologetically.

'Well, I'll be damned,' muttered Paul to Rose. 'I wonder what that blighter's been up to?'

Rose caught herself staring at them. So they were a foursome, then, and Leigh McDowie was with Tanya Dickenson, who had eyes only for him.

A feeling of utter weariness descended upon Rose, and she could hardly finish the meal. Her surroundings seemed to recede into a grey mist, and she could not follow what Paul was saying; she longed for solitude, the peace and privacy of her bed. All she could see was her mother's face, calm and smiling as she recounted her conversation with 'that lovely doctor wid his hair on his shoulders and a look in his eye'.

Rose awoke early on Monday morning, and lay listening to the dawn chorus of blackbirds and thrushes in the suburban gardens behind the little terraced house. A high, cloudless sky promised another scorchingly hot day, and her thoughts flew to her mother and the operation in a few hours' time, when, with her under the merciful oblivion of a general anaesthetic, Mr Horsfield would take away the invasive mass of enemy cells. Would Brigid then recover her strength again? Rose hardly dared to hope. She herself would not be allowed in the gynae theatre, but was detailed to assist Mr Rowan with Mrs Mowbray's Caesarean section, scheduled to begin at the same time.

At nine o'clock promptly Jane Mowbray was wheeled into the maternity theatre and gently placed on the slightly tilted operating table. Dr Okoje, the senior registrar in anaesthetics, had to maintain a delicate balance between the complex medication for the control of epilepsy and a level of unconsciousness not too deep to affect the infant about to be brought into the world five weeks before due time. The paediatric registrar, Dr Cranstone, was gowned and gloved ready to receive the premature baby and give immediate resuscitation as necessary before transferring it downstairs in a waiting incubator to the special care baby unit on the ground floor.

Mr Rowan was scrubbing up at the long washbasin, and Rose joined him there; Sister Dickenson was already scrubbed, gowned and preparing her instrument trolley, threading sutures and putting out the knife, dissecting forceps and artery clamps on the Mayo tray which could be adjusted to the surgeon's height and swivelled to any position required.

Auxiliary Nurse Beryl was runner, ready to fetch and carry for any of the staff engaged on the operation. The medical student Dan Clark was there to watch, while his friend Ben Davis was witnessing that other operation about to take place in the gynae theatre.

As Mr Rowan made the first incision along the bikini line, Rose drew a sharp intake of breath as she thought of the simultaneous incision being made by Mr Horsfield; his assistant was Leigh McDowie. Rose knew that she had to concentrate all her attention on Jane Mowbray, and she was thankful to have such a rewarding task during this time of anxiety — not like poor Mr Mowbray, biting his nails as he waited in the theatre annexe, plied with coffee and reassurance from Staff Midwife Moffatt.

It took only a few minutes for the surgeon to sever the layers of skin, muscle and shiny uterine wall, and to put his hand on the baby in its warm, moist, living nest. As Rose held the abdominal retractor, Mr Rowan deftly removed and held up a little boy, pink and slippery, and although undersized he gave a high, mewing cry as if protesting against being disturbed. His little legs jerked and his tiny fists clenched as Mr Rowan clamped and cut the umbilical cord and handed him to Dr Cranstone. A sigh of relief went up from all present; the silent tension was broken.

'A boy, and he seems to be in pretty good shape,' commented Dr Cranstone as he placed the baby in the heated resuscitation cot.

'At nine-seventeen precisely,' noted Rose.

'Syntometrine given,' said Dr Okoje.

'Go and tell the dad,' Tanya told the auxiliary. 'How much does the child weigh, Philip?'

'One point seven kilograms — that's — er — about three pounds, twelve ounces,' answered Dr Cranstone with satisfaction.

Over in the gynae theatre Mr Horsfield and Dr McDowie looked at each other above their surgical masks; and the consultant slowly shook his head before proceeding to do what he could.

In the much more relaxed atmosphere as she helped

Mr Rowan to close the severed layers with tiny stitches, Rose allowed her thoughts to return to her mother. Yesterday they had attended Mass together in the hospital chapel, where Brigid had made her confession and received absolution. Sister Kelly had tut-tutted at her patient's exhausted appearance on her return, but Rose had appreciated their quiet time of worship and Father Naylor's kindness. It had been a necessary part of Brigid's treatment, and she was now quite resigned to whatever Mr Horsfield might decide — plus the fact that Dr McDowie would be there at her side throughout the operation. It was strange, thought Rose, the closeness between her mother and that nonchalant doctor; what after all was Brigid to him, or he to Brigid? Yet Rose was grateful for the comfort he gave, for whatever reason.

At a quarter to ten Rose placed the adhesive dresing across the line of stitches, wiped her forehead and pulled off her cap. Mr Mowbray stepped forward eagerly as his wife was wheeled out of the theatre, and leaned over her sleeping face.

'We've got a son, Jane, and he's a little belter — I've seen him. Thank you, Janie, darling — '

Laurie Moffatt patted his shoulder and told him he could sit beside Jane in the postnatal ward, then, raising her voice slightly, she looked into the theatre and called to Rose.

'Dr Gillis! Could you go over to Gynae as soon as you've changed, please?'

Rose's face paled. 'You mean Gynae Theatre, Laurie?'

'No, Rose, Gynae Ward,' answered the big blonde with some embarrassment. 'Sister Kelly has telephoned for you.'

'You'd better go straight over, Rose,' said Mr Rowan quietly. 'Beryl, fetch Dr Gillis an iced lemonade while she's changing, will you? In fact we could all use one. Phew!'

Rose trembled as she threw off her green theatre gown and pulled on her light summer dress and white coat. She forgot to change her shoes, and ran all the way to Gynae in white theatre plimsolls.

Brigid lay on the bed in her room, an intravenous drip running into her right arm, a urine catheter draining into a plastic bag, and a wound drain connected to a vacuum bottle on the floor beside the bed. Sister Kelly was checking her blood-pressure, and Brigid's lids flickered. She turned her head, her unfocused eyes searching as she muttered incoherently.

'Rose. . .daughter. . .forgive me, forgive me.'

Rose took hold of her mother's hand and held it in both of hers.

'I'm here with you, Mummy. Don't try to talk.'

She had not said *Mummy* since she was a child.

'I'm sorry, little Rose,' whispered Brigid. 'Forgive me — oh, please forgive me.'

'Sh, Mummy. Everything's fine. I'm here, darling. I'm right here beside you,' repeated Rose in bewildered anguish.

'Forgive me, Rose. Forgive. . .'

The words tailed off and Brigid's eyelids closed as the effect of a strong pain-relieving injection of diamorphine began to take effect. Rose stood holding her mother's hand until the anxious muttering ceased.

'I'm sorry, Dr Gillis, love, it's just that she kept on saying your name,' apologised Sister Kelly. 'I thought maybe the sight of you would calm her.'

'Of course, Sister,' faltered Rose, her dark eyes

brimming. 'But what does she mean, Sister? Why is she asking me to forgive her? It's I who should ask her forgiveness for my carelessness, my lack of basic observation——'

Sister Kelly put a warning finger to her lips and glanced meaningfully at the patient. Rose bowed her head and covered her face with her hands.

And then suddenly she felt strong arms close around her, leading her out of the room, half carrying her along the corridor to the ward office. Blindly she clung to a white coat and buried her untidy dark head against a hard chest, aware that she was being held, supported and strengthened by the encircling arms.

'All right, Rose. All right, my love.'

In her deep distress it seemed quite natural that Leigh McDowie should be with her, comforting her and answering her questions.

'Why does she want me to forgive her? What for? *Why*?' she implored.

'Probably because she realises that you blame yourself because she didn't let you know how ill she was,' he said gently, 'though she may not remember a word of all this when she's properly round, so don't take it too seriously. Patients get funny ideas when they're surfacing from a GA. Leave her to sleep now, and talk with her later.'

'Why is she back from Theatre so soon?' she whispered against his coat lapels, still clinging to him like a child.

'Because the operation's over, my love,' he told her kindly and patiently as he stroked her dark hair, now collapsing from the neat coil she had pinned in place when she got up. 'Mr Horsfield will have a word with you when he's finished the list.'

'What's he going to tell me?' she demanded, drawing her head back and looking up into the brown eyes that were no longer teasing but softened with compassion. She saw pity in his face, pity for her mother and herself — and she read the truth without being told.

'He couldn't save her!' she cried. 'It's inoperable — oh, my God!'

Two strong fingers were placed firmly on her lips.

'Stop that, Rose. Stop it at once. You're going to have to be strong for her sake. She needs you, so be brave, my love.'

She drew a long, long sigh before looking him straight in the eyes and answering calmly, 'Yes, I'll try. Thank you.'

He released her as an auxiliary appeared with a tray of iced fruit squash, and the world reverted to something approximating to normal again.

When Mr Horsfield spoke to her at midday in his office, he found her surprisingly calm as she received the news she had already guessed.

'I've removed the uterus, ovaries, Fallopian tubes and every lymph gland I could see, but I'm afraid there's considerable spread, my dear,' he sighed. 'The wonder is that she's kept going for so long. You mustn't waste what time you have left in vain regrets, Rose — on the contrary, she'll need cheering and supporting. Happily you're near at hand to spend time with her, and whether she stays in hospital or goes home for a while, you've only to let me know your wishes. There'll be a bed for her whenever she needs it.'

Rose smiled mechanically as she framed the question that patients and relatives have asked from time immemorial.

'How long, Mr Horsfield?'

'Who can say? A month, perhaps, or maybe two or three. You know how impossible it is to predict these things, Rose. The important thing is to keep her as comfortable and contented as we can.'

'Yes, of course.'

Leigh's words came back to her. *'You're going to have to be strong. . . She needs you. . .'*

'Thank you, Mr Horsfield,' she said quietly.

'Take the rest of the day off, Rose.'

'Thank you, sir, but I'd rather not. I need to carry on as normal, and I can look in on my mother at any time of the day or night.'

'As you wish, my dear. Perhaps you're right,' he nodded. 'Life has to go on. I hear that the Mowbray baby is doing well so far — I went to see the mother in postnatal. She's so relieved to have it all over, poor girl, though of course she's quite heavily sedated at present.'

'Now to get the epilepsy under control again,' Rose ventured.

'Certainly. Thank heaven for phenytoin and all its derivatives — and the freedom to use them in a non-pregnant subject! I'll be glad of McDowie's opinion as to dosage during the stabilisation period. Her husband's going to have a heavy burden of responsibility, though.'

'I'm sure that's something he accepts, sir. I'd better be getting back to the department now. Thank you again for everything, sir.'

They shook hands without another word.

As Rose went through the ground-floor entrance to Maternity, which was at the rear of the main hospital building, Paul hurried after her and stopped her just inside the door. He looked flushed, and was obviously making an effort to calm himself.

'Darling, I've thought about you all the morning—fancy making you assist at that Caesarean when you've got all this worry! How's your mother?'

Rose returned his light kiss, and smiled wanly.

'Comfortable. She's on diamorphine, Paul.'

'Oh.' He understood the implication, and slipped his hand into hers, interlacing their fingers.

'And how are *you*, Paul?' she asked, sensing that there was something on his mind.

'Well, actually I'm hopping mad, Rose, and getting ready for a fight, and how! That bastard of a photographer!'

'Why, whatever's happened?' asked Rose, alarmed at the expression on his face.

'Wait till you see the evening paper today, with poor Caroline Trench's photograph plastered all over it for everybody to see the state she's in! Believe me, Rose, if this is Maynard's work, I shall personally kick his teeth in for him!'

'For heaven's sake don't do anything on impulse, Paul, and make sure you get your facts right before accusing Roger Maynard or anybody else,' she warned. 'Look, I've got to go now, I'm due to check on some antenatals before Mr Horsfield's ward round tomorrow. I'll catch up with you later, OK?'

She heard the animated talking and laughter in the antenatal ward office before she went in. Leigh McDowie and the senior midwife Sister Pardoe were looking at the newspaper that she had brought back with her after her lunch break.

'Whoever could have taken these?' she asked as Leigh McDowie whistled.

'They're good pictures, anyway, especially consider-ing the cloak-and-dagger circumstances,' he commented appraisingly. 'Hmm, not bad at all. Oh, hi, Rose—come and cast your beautiful eyes over these. What will your boyfriend say? Or did he take them himself and flog them to the paper on the quiet?'

On the front page was a picture of Caroline Trench sitting up in bed with a bandage round her head, and inside there were two more. One showed her lying full-length with her leg in plaster, the intravenous drip well in evidence; the other was a view of her face behind a bank of flowers, her wide eyes looking soulfully over the top of them. A nurse stood on either side of her, each with a hand on her shoulder.

'*Actress in Motorway Accident Horror*' was printed across the front page, while on the inside page the headline was '*Nurses in Bedside Vigil for Heartbreak Caroline*'.

'I just can't understand how any outside photographer could have taken these,' declared Sister Pardoe, a pleasant-faced Scotswoman in her late forties. 'I know Sister Banks on Female Surgical would never dream of allowing it! Sister Dickenson, have you seen today's paper?' she asked as Tanya came in, glancing quickly towards Leigh McDowie.

Rose noticed the look that passed between them, and she remembered the lively group of diners at the Old Barn on Saturday evening, and Roger Maynard's late arrival. She supposed he must have used his considerable charm on the night staff to allow him access to Caroline Trench's bedside.

'Her make-up's very tastefully applied, isn't it? remarked Leigh with a deadpan expression, and Tanya giggled quietly.

For Paul's sake Rose refused to join in the gossip and amusement, but her mouth tightened a little at the sight of the photographs. If they were anything to go by, the actress had hardly been coerced against her will to pose for them.

'Excuse me for interrupting, but I need to do a round of the antenatal mothers,' she said crisply. 'Have you the case-notes ready, Sister Dickenson? How's Mrs Lambert with the low-lying placenta? Her last scan showed that it was almost down to the cervix. Has she had any blood loss?'

'Obviously not, Doctor, or I'd have let the obstetric team know at once,' retorted Tanya with a toss of her silky silver-blonde head.

Rose stiffened, especially when she saw Leigh McDowie's quickly suppressed smile, and to her intense annoyance she felt her face and neck flushing hotly. Had she really clung to him desperately in the gynae ward office that morning, and felt his arms enfold her, and heard him whisper, 'Rose, my love' — could it actually have happened? She had better forget it, and soon.

# CHAPTER THREE

THE hot July days and nights went by, and Rose found plenty to occupy her mind during the long hours on call as senior house officer. Leigh McDowie was a reliable and cool-headed colleague who got his work done thoroughly without ever appearing to be in a hurry, though Rose was sometimes irritated by what she considered his laid-back attitude. In the antenatal ward with all its special problems and complications of pregnancy she found him decidedly helpful; the patients liked his easy humour, and he was quick to pick up signs of any changes in medical conditions.

'I'm not too happy about that poor Pendle kid, Rose,' he remarked one afternoon in the antenatal ward office, just one week after Brigid's operation.

'You mean Trish Pendle with the toxaemia,' nodded Rose. 'Yes, she hasn't got much going for her, has she? Only eighteen and deserted by her boyfriend, her parents separated—it's hardly surprising that she gave in to the first boy who showed her any attention—the usual story.'

Tanya Dickenson interposed sharply.

'Trish Pendle would do better to stay in bed and rest instead of always hopping off to the day-room and smoking like a chimney,' she declared. 'She's such a *silly* girl—I mean, she refuses to take her iron tablets because she says they disagree with her, and yet she gets a girlfriend to bring her in a huge packet of soggy chips every night—no wonder she's overweight!'

'I'll try having a talk with her,' said Rose, 'and we'll get the dietician up to see her and discuss her likes and dislikes. Meanwhile I'll write her up for a different iron preparation in liquid syrup.'

'Her blood-pressure's creeping up, Leigh,' Tanya went on. 'A hundred and forty over ninety-five this morning, and she's got one plus of protein in her urine. What that girl needs is a twice-daily dose of methyldopa to slow her down, keep her in bed and control her blood-pressure.'

'I'll talk to Mr Horsfield about her on his ward-round tomorrow,' said Rose briefly. She was irritated by Sister Dickenson's self-assumed role as diagnostician and prescriber of medication.

'And let's get a scan done before the old man's round,' added Leigh. 'Can you book it for this afternoon, Tanya?'

'A scan?' queried Rose. 'She had one last week, and it showed a thirty-six-week gestation. There's no point in doing another so soon.'

'Do you want me to try to get one done, Leigh?' asked Tanya, ignoring Rose. 'I doubt if the scan department can fit her in this afternoon at such short notice, unless we say it's urgent.'

'Yeah, we'll call it an emergency,' he told her. 'Speak to them in your most seductive tones, Tanya — and before you beam your killer rays on to me, Rose, I mean a renal scan.'

'Whatever for? There's no sign of kidney failure,' objected Rose.

'I think there could be more to Trish's problems than just toxaemia,' said Leigh thoughtfully. 'Just a hunch. Put her on four-hourly temperature recording, Tanya, and a strict fluid balance chart. We'll see if anything interesting shows up. All right by you, Rose?'

Rose could hardly contradict him, as he had practised as a physician for the past two years, and she knew that Mr Horsfield respected his opinions. She nodded her assent.

'Lynne Westbrook is just as sad a girl in a different way,' he continued, picking up another set of case-notes.

'The one with twins due in September? Yes, but wouldn't you have expected more sense from a girl of her background?' queried Rose with a frown. 'An intelligent young woman with an academic mind, only just graduated with a science degree from Manchester University, and a really promising future before her — except for this!'

'These university Christmas parties can be just as wild as hospital ones,' commented Leigh drily. 'Though *twins* does seem to be a bit over the top, yes.'

'I can't help feeling extremely sorry for her,' said Tanya. 'Apparently the boyfriend's an Arts graduate without a penny to his name, and wanted her to have an abortion. When she refused, he went off on a round-the-world hike.'

'That figures. They're all doing it these days, because there aren't any jobs for BAs,' shrugged Leigh.

'The poor girl must have had a bad time telling her parents,' went on Tanya. 'It seems they're very *county*, and live in some crumbling old mansion in the wilds of Dorset.'

'Hell of a blow for them,' muttered Leigh.

'At least there shouldn't be too much of a problem getting the babies adopted,' said Tanya. 'Our social worker Mrs McClennan has been up to see Lynne, and says there are lots of infertile couples desperate to adopt, and would accept twins.'

'Quite an undertaking,' observed Leigh, and Rose suddenly thought of Grace and Alfred Bradshaw who had been in the motorway accident.

'Come on, Dr McDowie, we'd better go down to Postnatal now,' she said. 'It's important that we follow up all our delivered mothers.'

The postnatal ward was situated on the ground floor, adjoining the special care baby unit. The heat seemed even more oppresive downstairs, although all the windows were open. Sister Dorothy Beddows, a plump, motherly Jamaican woman who usually wore a broad smile, seemed a little out of sorts, though she enquired after Mrs Gillis with genuine concern, and slipped a little hand-crocheted cross into Rose's pocket before escorting the two doctors round her ward.

Fretful babies whimpered, and the mothers looked tired and harassed as they sat around on their beds, each with a cot at the end. Rose was aware of an unsettled atmosphere in the hitherto smoothly run ward, which was divided into a ten-bedded unit and three smaller ones each with four beds. In one of these was Jane Mowbray, the only patient who was smiling. Her son Luke had been transferred from the special care unit, and she was giving him a bottle-feed.

'Of course I'd have liked to breast-feed, Doctor, but I knew I couldn't because of the epilepsy and all the drugs I'm on,' she told Rose. 'Isn't he *adorable*? And he weighs four pounds one ounce now!'

Rose duly complimented Jane on the small but healthy-looking baby boy, who was vigorously sucking at the bottle.

'He'll soon put on weight if he goes on like *that*!' she laughed. 'No problems, Jane?'

'None at all. No fits since the op, I'm up and walking around, taking showers and feeling great,' the happy mother reported, but there was an undercurrent of resentment among the other three mothers in the ward; on a pretext of studying Mrs Mowbray's case-notes, Rose discreetly listened to the conversation between them while Leigh chatted with Sister Beddows about the progress of her own daughter's first pregnancy.

'If I want to put my baby on the bottle, I'm jolly well going to, no matter what they say,' muttered one of the mothers, a young girl of about twenty.

'You can give your baby second-best if you insist on doing so, but I intend to breast-feed my son, and I won't allow any of those night nurses to give him a bottle,' declared another mother in the firm tones of a schoolteacher. Mrs Gainsford had gone to the same convent school as Rose, but about ten years earlier: she had just had her first baby at thirty-seven.

'That's easy for you to say, but none of us had a wink of sleep in here last night because of your baby hollering for hours on end!' retorted the third patient, a forthright Lancashire housewife and mother of three. 'What this place needs is a decent-sized nursery where the babies can be taken every night to give us the chance of a proper rest. They used to have one when I was in before, and it was heaven just to get a good night's sleep.'

She caught sight of Rose's questioning look, and raised her voice defiantly. 'And I don't mind who hears me say so! Damned ridiculous idea, keeping the babies in the ward all night.'

'But surely you'll have your baby beside you when you go home?' ventured Rose with a smile.

'Oh, aye, but I'll only have my own, won't I?' the mother pointed out. 'I won't have to listen to *her* poor starving nine-pounder bawling his head off for a proper feed!'

'How dare you say that?' Mrs Gainsford almost shouted. 'Don't you know that it's only by frequent stimulation that the milk increases to satisfy the baby's needs? Women like you two deny your babies their natural birthright just because you're not prepared to persevere and put up with a temporary inconvenience!'

Tears of anger and frustration welled up in her eyes, and Sister Beddows hastily interposed.

'Now, now, ladies, we don't want any arguments,' she said firmly, though not unsympathetically. 'We're all different in our attitudes, and must learn to tolerate each other's ideas, give and take, live and let live! You all have beautiful babies, so can't you just be thankful for them? Let's have some harmony between ourselves, shall we?'

By including herself in the plea for compromise, she managed to avoid an out-and-out row between the mothers, but Rose could see how upset the good-humoured sister was, and Leigh too had overheard the heated exchange. He nodded encouragement towards the determined breast-feeder.

'Good on you, Mrs Gainsford, you're doing a great job,' he assured her. 'Give him the good stuff, and he'll really go for it as soon as he gets the knack!'

An ear-splitting yell went up from the hungry baby, who had just been settled in his cot.

'Look, my dear, let me try giving him a little sterile

water,' suggested Sister Beddows soothingly. 'He may be just thirsty in all this heat.'

'I don't want him to be offered any bottles at all,' Mrs Gainsford insisted. 'He's to have nothing but me.'

'Well, I'm sorry, love, but in that case you'll have to pick him up and put him to the breast again,' said the Jamaican sister patiently. 'He can't go on yelling like this, can he? Are you drinking plenty of water? You need to get through at least four jugs a day to produce enough milk. You heard about the miracle when the water was turned into wine? Well, this is an even older miracle, you see.'

She smiled, and Mrs Gainsford blinked back her tears as she took her baby from the sister's arms, and Rose pulled the curtains round her bed.

'What on earth's the matter, Dorothy?' Rose asked point-blank when the three of them were back in the postnatal ward office. 'Is it the heat that's getting them down?'

The sister's broad face was tense and unsmiling; she gave a sigh and shook her head with a touch of exasperation.

'I just hate to see my mothers unhappy, Rose, and yet I don't know what I can do to improve matters without a big row,' she explained in her pleasantly deep West Indian accent. 'And especially I don't want to grumble to *you*, with all the worry you've got over your dear mother——'

'Then grumble to *me*, Sister, and then I won't feel so left out of things,' suggested Leigh, putting an arm around her ample waist. 'Lay your head on my shoulder and tell me all about it!'

Dorothy Beddows had to smile in spite of herself, and Rose silently noted that he took as much trouble to charm a middle-aged woman as a young and attractive girl like Tanya. Another conquest, she thought to herself.

'It's Philip Cranstone,' said Dorothy with reluctance, and both of them looked at her in surprise. Dr Cranstone had been at Beltonshaw General for some time, and had won all hearts as a paediatric houseman. On promotion to registrar, he had married a young staff midwife, and they were now the proud parents of a young baby son. They were also personal friends of Dorothy Beddows.

'Go on, Dorothy, what's the trouble?' prompted Rose.

'Don't say Philip's been making improper suggestions to Lil,' grinned Leigh, referring to a surly domestic who always seemed to be mopping the floor of Postnatal. Rose frowned at him, and he winked back at her.

'You know that Dr Cameron has gone out to Ethiopia for three months with a team of relief workers?' said Dorothy, and they nodded. The eminent consultant paediatrician's mercy mission had been headlined in the media, and also the fact that Dr Cranstone would deputise in his absence.

'It's given Philip a chance to implement his "Breast is Best" campaign,' went on Dorothy. 'Every mother is expected to feed her baby while she's in hospital.'

'Quite right too,' commented Leigh. 'It's what breasts are for, isn't it? I'd have thought you'd support his crusade, Sister! Best for the baby, a free supply that's always handy, no risk of infection, and gives the baby immunity—straight out of *Successful Breastfeeding*, published by the Royal College of Midwives!'

'You've forgotten to say that it binds the mother and

baby together in a special relationship,' observed Rose drily.

'That's right, Rose—the ultimate orgasm,' he nodded back, his eyes dancing. She looked away.

'So what's going wrong, Dorothy?' she asked seriously.

'Just the difference between theory and practice,' replied the midwife. 'Believe me, I've worked with maternity patients for long enough to know that nothing is ever quite as simple and straightforward as it's supposed to be! There are some mothers—and Annette Cranstone is one of them—who put the baby to the breast straight away and feed like a dream from day one, but many of them find it very difficult for all sorts of reasons, and a lot just don't want to do it.'

'Isn't it part of a midwife's job to encourage them, give them the right advice and help them to fix the little nipper on?' asked Leigh, genuinely interested. 'I mean, if a woman can only get started with feeding her baby, she'll come to realise all the benefits, won't she?'

'The trouble is that we now live in a very complex and artificial society, and it just doesn't work for all of them,' replied Dorothy. 'Women don't meekly do as they're told these days—they've got their own ideas, and they tell *us*! It's the reason why I don't wear myself out any more, trying to get a baby to suck when I know the mother doesn't intend to carry on with it. I save myself for the ones who really want to succeed, and I can tell the true from the false as soon as they arrive on the postnatal ward from the delivery unit! Mrs Gainsford is sincere, but she's encountering a lot of difficulty that she wasn't prepared for, and it's upsetting her. A big, hungry baby like that could do with an occasional formula feed to tide him over for a day or two, but even if she agreed, Philip would hit the roof when he saw the feeding chart.' She sighed and shrugged.

Rose did not feel inclined to disagree with a well-experienced midwife, but Leigh was unconvinced by the sister's argument.

'It's all too easy for them to give artificial feeds with all these bottles of milk hanging around, and the advertising of the various brands,' he remarked a little irritably. 'In the past women fed their babies because the only alternative was unsterilised cow's milk. There are too many choices now!'

'In the past rich women used poor mothers to suckle their babies for them,' retorted Dorothy, 'and their own babies had to go short! And if a mother died in childbirth, as all too often happened, some babies *did* survive on cow's milk. I did myself,' she added sadly.

Rose noticed the shadow that fell across her face, and decided that this conversation had gone on for long enough.

'We'll have to look into the problem, and perhaps have a joint discussion between the obstetric and paediatric teams,' she said. 'I'll mention the matter to Mr Horsfield.'

'Aren't you taking this all a bit far, Rosie?' asked Leigh in his infuriating way. 'Phil Cranstone's an excellent paediatrician, and now that he's become a daddy himself, he'll be getting plenty of first-hand experience — changing a few nappies and bathing the son and heir — and of course he'll be watching his lady wife feeding——'

'That's no help to my mothers, not if he expects them all to be like Annette Cranstone,' cut in Dorothy Beddows. 'Not many women are as pampered and cherished as she is, and they don't live in beautiful houses and have daily help with the housework — no way! You forget that every mother is a different indiviual.'

'And so is every baby,' added Rose.

'And what's right for one may not be ideal for another. You heard those three women talking just now,' insisted Dorothy.

'Well, I think you're both getting too overheated about this,' Leigh told them. 'Cranstone's in touch with all the latest research, and we must keep an open mind — '

He was totally unprepared for their reaction.

'If that isn't the limit of male chauvinist thought!' exclaimed Rose.

'Typical of a man,' echoed Dorothy.

'Oh, come off it, girls, be reasonable, give Cranstone's theories a trial at least!' he protested, though he found his attention drawn to Rose's blazing deep blue eyes; the thought came to him that they were exactly the colour of violets. . .quite enchanting.

'You've made up my mind, Dr McDowie,' she told him contemptuously. 'I shall certainly ask Mr Horsfield to arrange an early meeting with Dr Cranstone and some of the senior midwives — '

'And some of the mothers too,' Dorothy added.

'Certainly, they're the most important ones involved, with the babies,' agreed Rose. '*You* may be content to take orders from a paediatrician about postnatal care, Doctor, but I'm damned sure that *I'm* not.'

She turned her back on him, and spoke to the sister.

'Leave this with me, Dorothy. I'm just as concerned as you are about keeping our mothers happy, and I'll have a word with Mr Horsfield tomorrow, OK?'

'Thanks, Rose. I knew I could count on you,' answered the Jamaican woman gratefully. 'But I don't really want to fall out with Philip — or with you, Dr McDowie. It's just that the mothers have to come first with me and my midwives.'

'That's all right, Sister, I'm all in favour of keeping women happy by whatever means are possible,' answered Leigh with what Rose felt to be insufferable condescension. 'In fact, if you two experts will excuse me now, I've got a pressing engagement with a very special lady, and I mustn't keep her waiting.'

He waved away the tray of tea and iced fruit juice that a nursing auxiliary had set down on the office desk.

'No, thanks, I haven't time. It's my evening off. Enjoy your night on call, Rose, and don't use up too much nervous energy — bye!'

And he was gone without a backward glance.

'Thank heaven for that!' cried Rose emphatically. 'Sister Dickenson is more than welcome to his company. Our friend Dr McDowie has a lot to learn about women and their special needs.'

'Maybe so,' replied Sister Beddows with an odd little sideways look. 'And *you*, Dr Gillis, are going to teach him.'

Rose seemed to be fated not to see her mother that evening. Every time she attempted to visit, she was interrupted. At five o'clock a thirteen-week miscarriage was admitted to the gynae ward, and needed to go to Theatre for a complete evacuation of the uterus under a general anaesthetic. Mr Rowan allowed Rose to perform this operation, as he had seen her do several D and Cs, and was satisfied with her technique.

At six-thirty she was called to the delivery unit to inspect and repair an episiotomy done by a staff midwife who had supervised Ben Davis, one of the medical students, as he conducted his third normal delivery. The mother was a pleasant primigravida in her twenties, and her husband was overjoyed by the arrival of his baby daughter.

'It was a tremendous moment, Dr Gillis,' breathed Ben Davis, flushed and bright-eyed after his achievement. 'I'd hung around talking to the couple all this afternoon, and helped Dr Okoje to start an epidural anaesthetic for her. Then when she was in second stage and pushing for all she was worth, I really felt as if——' He hesitated, unable to find the right words.

'As if you were actually in control of the situation?' prompted Rose, a little amused at his enthusiasm.

'Something like that, yes. And the midwife was so good—you know, she watched every move, but she let me get on with the delivery. Some of the midwives don't give us a chance to get our hands on! After she'd done the episiotomy, I controlled the baby's head as it rotated and emerged, and I felt this loop of cord around its neck——'

'Oh, lord! Did you manage to pull it over the head?' asked Rose.

'No, I couldn't, it was too tight. But no panic, I just automatically reached for the clamps and cord scissors, and cut it. It was all so *marvellous*, Rose, really it was!'

He smiled triumphantly and drew his green-sleeved arm across his moist forehead. 'Phew! Do you know, I think I'm going to enjoy obstetrics after all! I don't want to sound sloppy, but it really is a privilege to be present at the very moment of—er—and the husband kept calling me "Doctor"—it felt so strange, Rose—er Dr Gillis.'

She smiled indulgently at his raptures over the work which many students found overwhelming, even shocking in its stark intimacy when they were first confronted by a woman in labour. She invited him to watch her repairing the episiotomy, the careful layered stitching together of the delicate tissue.

'This is a tiresome business for a newly delivered mother to have to endure,' she explained, 'but a well-repaired episiotomy can save a lot of gynaecological problems in later life. A weakened pelvic floor leads to prolapse and all sorts of discomfort and embarrassment.' She thought sadly of her own mother as she spoke.

When the suturing was completed, Rose went to the office to write a brief report of it; Staff Nurse Laurie Moffatt was in charge of the antenatal ward, which shared the office with the delivery unit.

'Oh, Dr Gillis, I've got something interesting to show you!' she said, brandishing a pink slip of paper which Rose recognised as an ultra-sonic scan report. 'It's Trish Pendle's, done this afternoon—just look at *that*!'

Rose picked it up, and rapidly read the handwritten report which sported a red stick-on star for urgent attention.

Left kidney small, poorly outlined, appears to be non-functioning, suggestive of congenital abnormality or chronic pyelo-nephritis. Right kidney shows moderate hydro-nephrois due to reflux.

Rose stared at the words in consternation. So Leigh McDowie's hunch had been right: the girl had a chronic kidney condition, possibly from before birth, and her good kidney had to do the work of two; so far it had managed, but the additional strain of pregnancy, aggravated by a poor diet, was proving too great a burden, and it was beginning to show signs of pressure and a backward flow of urine. The warning signs of rising blood-pressure, swollen ankles and protein in the urine had been diagnosed as toxaemia of pregnancy, a fairly common condition. It was too soon for the newly commenced temperature and fluid balance charts to add any useful information, but Rose went straight to find Trish Pendle and ask her to get into bed for a careful examination.

'Just sit up for me, Trish,' she requested. 'Now, does it hurt *here*, my dear?' She gently pressed her palm against the girl's loin, to the left of the spine, over the faulty kidney.

'Ooh! Er—no, not much,' mumbled Trish, pleased to have some attention shown to her.

'Or here, Trish? What about *here*?' asked Rose, carefully pressing her palm to the right of the spine.

'*Ouch*! Yeah, that's sore—*ow*!' protested Trish. 'Yeah, I been telling 'em it aches there, but nobody takes any notice, they just say it's 'cos of the baby.'

Rose was concerned. Tenderness in the right loin indicated that the back pressure was causing some inflammation of the good kidney, already overloaded with work.

''Ere, 'ave you 'eard anything about that scan I 'ad this afternoon?' demanded Trish suspiciously.

'Yes, my dear, and it does look as if you might have a bit of kidney trouble,' answered Rose with the cool, kind manner she used for imparting unwelcome news.

'What are they going to do about it, then? Will Dr Horsfield start me off early?' asked the girl hopefully.

'I really couldn't say right now, Trish; we'll have to wait and see what he says on the ward round tomorrow,' Rose temporised. 'Meanwhile we'll get some more tests done. Don't worry about it — you're in the right place — and that reminds me, Sister tells us that you're having some problems with the food here — '

By the time Rose had finished reassuring Trish and advising her about diet, it was visiting time; she realised that she was quite hungry, having had nothing but drinks since lunch. She decided to go to the mess and postpone her visit to her mother until tucking-down time.

Paul Sykes was drinking a solitary cup of coffee, and Rose made her way towards his table with her tray of tuna salad and a roll.

'Darling, you look done in,' he sympathised as she sat down. 'What you need is a proper break — we'll definitely go to Nethersedge this weekend.'

'But Paul, how can I? Mother will be discharged home later this week — '

'Good heavens, Rose, you've only got to ask Derek Horsfield to keep her in over the weekend!' he protested. 'You'll need a couple of days' rest before all the hassle of trying to look after her at home while working here for hours at a stretch. It's going to be a hell of an undertaking, you know.'

'Yes, Paul, I do know.' Rose lowered her eyes and experienced a chill of dismay over her divided loyalties. During the past ten days she had come to realise how much she owed to her mother, and how deep was the love between them, even though they had not been demonstrably close. Now sorrowfully aware that the sands of life were running low for Brigid and would soon be through, Rose not only owed her mother every minute that she could spare, but she truly wanted to show a daughter's devotion while there was still time. There was no question about it: her mother took precedence over Paul.

'Let's talk about something else,' she said deliberately. 'I saw Caroline Trench on ITN this evening — one of the antenatal patients had a little portable. She looked very glamorous! Has Roger Maynard been scaling the drainpipes again?'

There was a slightly mischievous glint in Rose's eyes. Paul's indignation over the invasion of his patient's privacy had been hastily swallowed when the actress's love of publicity became apparent. Television cameras had followed in the wake of Maynard's early visit, and stories of Caroline's amusing sayings were being passed round the hospital daily.

Paul chuckled. 'Ah, yes, I made the mistake of assuming that Caroline was just another mortal like the rest of us. Oh, Rose, what a woman! What a character! She's so interested in everybody, and keeps the other patients entertained all the time. They're going to miss her terribly when she goes out.'

'Which will presumably be earlier than you thought?' surmised Rose.

'No, she'll be in till mid-August at least,' he told her. 'The tib and fib were shattered to splinters, and it was tricky work putting them all together. I'm concerned about what the leg's going to look like when the plaster comes off — at worst, it could mean another operation, or even two.' He shook his head, and Rose could see how worried he was about the all-important appear-ance of an actress's leg.

'She's got youth and health on her side, plus an obvious determination to get back to normal,' she reminded him with a smile, and he nodded emphatically.

'She surely has! That girl's turned Female Surgical into an ongoing party, day and night!'

Rose silently registered that Caroline had recovered very quickly from the death of her boyfriend, and wondered if his wife was doing as well; but she kept these thoughts to herself.

She finished her meal, glanced at her watch and said she had better be going; in actual fact she went to her room in the residency to lie down for half an hour, trying to relax her mind and body before a night on call, and in minutes she fell fast asleep.

It was a quarter to ten when Rose entered the gynae ward, and finding her mother's room empty, she walked into the main twenty-bedded unit, only to discover that almost every bed had lost its occupant. There were no staff around, and no sign of the drinks trolley, usually in evidence at this time. Only today's post-ops were sleeping off the effects of their anaes-thetics as Rose walked down the ward, drawn by the sound of a man's voice singing. . .

And through the glass partition doors that led on to the balcony at the end of the ward, Rose saw her mother sitting in a circle of women in dressing-gowns, aged from twenty to over seventy, plus the staff nurse and auxiliary on night duty, all listening entranced to a dark-eyed man with hair down to his shoulders; he wore an open-necked shirt and cotton trousers as he sat playing a guitar accompaniment to his own deliciously saucy English rendering of an old French song. The ladies giggled with delight as he described a closed horse-drawn cab bowling along a cobbled Parisian street, and the couple within exchanging kisses; then he sang in French, with plenty of '*Ooh, là, là*'s and clip-clop sounds of the horses' hoofs. The guitar wittily echoed the words in a rhythmic plink-plonk, plink-plonk, and Leigh winked wickedly as the sound gradually faded into silence. . .

His admiring audience burst into laughter and applause.

'Oooh, you ought to be on telly, Dr McDowie!' gasped a large lady, holding a supportive hand over her operation scar. 'You'll have us all bursting our stitches!'

'Let's have something quieter, then,' he suggested, plucking a few introductory chords on the strings, slowly and dreamily. Rose stepped back a few paces, not wanting to interrupt the entertainment. A silence settled on the group in the warm twilight as his clear, firm voice rose on the scented air that wafted across from the rose-beds edging the grassy expanse beyond the balcony.

'O, my Luve's like a red red rose
That's newly sprung in June ——'

Sighs of contented oohs and aahs greeted the opening lines as the ladies settled to listen to this most haunting of love-songs. Rose stood absolutely still, not daring to move. She caught sight of her mother's face, intent and rapt, the transparent skin touched by a faint pink glow on her cheeks, the tendrils of silky white hair like a halo around her head. The beauty of the moment seemed to hold a message for Rose — of comfort, reassurance and a certainty that she would be upheld during the testing time ahead. She stole a glance at Leigh's face, and saw the tenderness as he lowered his voice to sing very softly, just for Brigid.

'I will love thee still, my Dear,
While the sands o' life shall run.'

A blackbird was singing somewhere above them as the song ceased, and this time there was no applause. Several ladies hastily wiped their eyes, and Rose bit her lip. Should she creep softly away now, without revealing herself?

'Rose! Oh, Rose, me girl, sure I thought ye were never comin' to see me today!'

A chorus of greetings followed her mother's words, and she smiled as she stepped on to the balcony; she found it difficult to meet Leigh's eye, remembering how they had parted in Postnatal that afternoon.

'Oh, Dr Gillis, he's *magic*!' swooned a young girl who had had a D and C for heavy periods.

'You should have heard him sing *Memories*!' cried a housewife who had had an ovarian cyst removed.

Rose was furious at herself for blushing, but Leigh came to her rescue.

'Tell her your news, Brigid, me darlin',' he said.

'Wait till I tell ye, Rose—I've had a letter from me sister Maura, and what d'ye think she says? She's comin' over to stay for a bit—isn't that grand? Just until I get back on me feet, like. It'll save ye a lot o' worry, Rose, bein' as busy as ye are!'

Rose looked lovingly at her mother's animated face as she linked arms with her to assist with the slow walk back to Brigid's room. Aunt Maura's visit would certainly solve a lot of problems, and Rose was moved to see how happy her mother was at the prospect of seeing her sister again after so long.

When she had said goodnight and switched off the bed-lamp, Rose did a quick round of the post-op gynae patients, and on reaching the end of the ward she saw that Leigh was lingering on the balcony; he beckoned to her, and she joined him. The patients had been recalled to their beds by the staff nurse who was doing the night medicine round, and she and he were alone.

'I told you I had a pressing engagement with a very special lady,' he reminded her.

She held out her hands. 'What can I say, Leigh? Your visits give her so much pleasure — and all the other patients in here, seemingly!'

He laughed softly, but then his features took on a more sombre air.

'It's good news about her sister coming over, and it eases the problem about sending her home — but you do realise that she'll probably have to come back in again, Rose, don't you? And it could be soon.'

He searched her face with concern, reluctant to discourage her, but not wanting her to have any false hopes about Brigid's condition.

'I know. Mr Horsfield has explained everything,' she replied steadily.

'Good girl.' There was a silence, and Rose decided to tell him about Trish Pendle's scan report and her own findings on examination.

'You were right about her, Leigh,' she admitted.

He shook his head gravely. 'The poor kid will need to be thoroughly investigated after delivery. We can't do an intravenous pyelogram X-ray now, but we can do a blood profile for urea, electrolytes, creatinine clearance and so on — and watch for bugs in the urine.'

She nodded. 'I've sent in the requests to the lab.'

He smiled approvingly. 'Good! Do you think the old man will go for an early delivery?'

'An early Caesarean, I'd guess,' she said. 'Her condition is only going to worsen while she's pregnant, isn't it?'

Leigh sighed. 'Oh, it just isn't fair, Rose — that poor kid! Whatever kind of a future has she got? Kidney dialysis? Kidney transplant? And the poor little beggar inside her, who's going to take *him* on? Believe me, Rose, there are times when I wish I'd gone into the theatre — I mean the other sort of theatre — it's what I wanted to do at one time!'

'Am I supposed to be glad or sorry that you didn't?' she asked, her face deliberately expressionless. He shot her a quick glance, then laughed out loud.

'Just think! I could be giving free matinees for pensioners and the disabled, Dr Gillis!'

'Like just now, Dr McDowie?'

'You're coming on, Dr Gillis.'

'A girl can but try, Dr McDowie.'

Rose felt herself warming to this man who happily spent his precious evening off serenading a group of gynae patients, and could also feel such a depth of sympathy for an overweight, under-educated unmarried mum.

'A lot of people have an over-romantic picture of maternity departments, Leigh,' she said conversationally, 'but *we* know that it isn't all rejoicing over the births of bonny babies! And yet I hadn't the heart to disillusion that dear boy Ben Davis this evening when he was in raptures over his third delivery! He was quite touching, really.'

'That young man's a good bet for the future,' Leigh

remarked. 'In fact, he could be another Mr Horsfield in twenty years' time. Let's learn from him, Rose.'

She did not understand. 'Who, Ben?'

'Yes, love. Don't let's forget our own early enthusiasm, the agony and the ecstasy over those first deliveries. I don't think that Ben will ever lose the sense of wonder, that's why he's so good—he'll never think he's learned it all. We're all students in this game, Rosie, and never stop learning. God help us if we do!'

'And our patients!' she added, surprised by his unusually thoughtful brown eyes that seemed to be searching into her very heart.

And suddenly they were close together, and he had taken hold of her hand. For a timeless moment they stood in a shared world of their own on the balcony in the gathering dusk. . .

The peep-peep-peep-peep of the electronic bleep in her pocket recalled her to the real world, and she turned away to answer its summons.

Leigh watched her walking quickly up the ward until she had disappeared from his sight.

# CHAPTER FOUR

'HAD you forgotten about the two new admissions for induction of labour tomorrow, Dr Gillis?' asked Staff Nurse Pat Kelsey, the red-haired young midwife in charge of the antenatal ward at night. 'It's nearly half-past ten, so I wondered if you intend to examine and assess them tonight?'

'Oh, Staff, I'm sorry,' apologised Rose. 'I was — er — rather delayed on Gynae this evening, but I know I should have come up earlier than this.'

'I thought you'd forgotten,' said Pat, though the disapproval in her voice was softened by sympathy. 'I'd have reminded you, but I guessed you'd be with your mother.'

'Is it too late to see them now?' asked Rose, hastily thumbing through the two sets of csae-notes that Pat had left out on the desk.

The first patient that Rose examined was already on the verge of labour, and the cervix was dilated to two centimetres. It was her second baby, ten days overdue.

'Splendid! You'll probably go into labour during the night, so you won't need to have an induction,' Rose told her with a smile.

'I hope you're right, Doctor,' said the woman anxiously. 'I don't fancy having my waters broken and a drip put up. I'd much rather go into labour naturally.'

'Don't worry, there's every chance that you will,' Rose assured her. 'Let's see the other lady now, Staff.'

On examining the other patient, Rose decided to

insert a tiny vaginal suppository containing a hormone preparation that would soften the tightly closed cervix overnight, making conditions more favourable for an induction of labour the next day.

'That's OK by me, Doctor. I asked Mr Horsfield if I could be started off a bit early because it's my mum's fiftieth birthday next week, and we're having a bit of a do,' confided the patient with engaging frankness. 'My sister's coming all the way from New Zealand for it, and I want her to see the baby before she goes back! It'll be her first nephew or niece.'

Rose smiled, noting that Mr Horsfield had written 'raised blood pressure' as the reason for early induction of labour, though it was no higher than might be expected in a heavily pregnant lady during a heatwave.

'Good! Now Staff Nurse Kelsey will put you on the monitor for a while, and then you can settle down to sleep,' Rose told her. 'You may need another prostin suppository tomorrow, otherwise we'll go ahead and break your waters, put up a drip and——'

'Oh, I don't mind what you do, Doctor, just as long as it's born in time!' exclaimed the cheerfully expectant mother as Pat attached the sensor which recorded the baby's heartbeat, a rapid double sound, pat-a-pat-a-pat-a-pat-a, on the monitor, sweet music to the mother's ears.

'Any problems on the delivery unit?' asked Rose when they returned to the office.

'Nothing that we midwives can't deal with, Dr Gillis,' answered Night Sister Grierson, a briskly efficient woman in her thirties who was deputising for the night nursing officer. 'One patient has just delivered, and there'll probably be another within the hour. No problem!'

'I shouldn't be surprised if one of the new admissions goes into labour,' remarked Rose. 'Don't forget to bleep the medical student on call, will you, Sister?'

'No need to, he's already here,' replied the midwife. 'Nice to have students who are prepared to spend time getting to know the patient beforehand. Dr McDowie sets them a good example, and it makes life a lot easier all round, especially for the mothers.'

Sister Angela Grierson was not usually free with compliments, and Rose noted Dr McDowie's name again. He seemed to be everybody's favourite in Maternity, and her heart gave an odd little lurch as she recalled his look and the touch of his hand when they had stood together on the balcony of Gynae in the warm semi-darkness. Suppose Staff Kelsey had not sent out the bleep summons to her at that moment, what would have happened next? What would he have said to her as he looked deep into her upturned face? She gave herself a shake. It was all due to his fondness for her mother, of course; those two were so unaccountably close!

She refused the offer of a drink from the auxiliary, and retired to her room in the residency, where she dozed for a couple of hours before being summoned to see an admission on the delivery unit.

'Only thirty-five weeks, and says she's getting regular pains,' Sister Grierson said over the telephone. 'Slightly raised temperature, and says she's been passing urine very frequently for the last two days, in other words she's got a urinary tract infection — but I have to ask you to see her because of her prematurity. She's convinced that she's in prem labour, but the monitor doesn't show any real contractions.'

Rose found that Sister Grierson's provisional diagnosis coincided exactly with her own. She was able to reassure the patient and her anxious boyfriend that premature delivery was most unlikely.

'We'll keep you in for a few days, and start you on a course of antibiotics as soon as we've sent a specimen of your urine to the lab,' she said calmly. 'Meanwhile you can have pain-killing tablets and a light sedative to help you settle.'

'Won't that affect the baby?' asked the patient, by no means convinced that she was not in labour. 'I mean, the poor little thing's so *small*, isn't it?'

The boyfriend immediately advised her to take whatever was being offered, and Rose left them to say goodbye to each other while she went to enquire about the situation in the delivery unit.

'No problems! Ben had his fourth delivery just before midnight, and Staff Kelsey has transferred that new admission over to me, the one you thought might come off—she's just having a hot bath,' reported Angela Grierson, bristling with efficiency.

'Good, she wanted to start off on her own,' nodded Rose. 'Nobody else in labour? You'll be able to get some knitting done tonight, Sister!'

'No chance! I'm on my own upstairs at present,' snapped the midwife. 'I've sent Staff Kelsey and the auxiliary down to Postnatal to help poor Sister Hicks. It's absolute pandemonium again tonight.'

'Really? Aren't the mothers and babies asleep?' asked Rose in surprise. It was just after two o'clock.

'Don't make me laugh! Could *you* sleep in a full ward where every mother has a new baby beside her?' demanded Sister Grierson. 'It's all right for you medical staff, you don't see the postnatal ward at night—or hear it! It's the midwives who have to try to put the doctors' wonderful theories into practice, while all *our* practical experience counts for nothing.'

Rose remembered Dorothy Beddow's comments the previous afternoon.

'Don't ever say that, Sister Grierson,' she said quickly. 'All of us on the obstetric team know that we rely on the midwives to keep the department going. It couldn't function without your round-the-clock care.'

'You may say that *now*, but when you get to be registrar or even a consultant one day, you'll forget what it's like at bedside level, just like Dr Philip Cranstone,' retorted Angela. 'He's a prime example of an idealist who thinks he can run the postnatal ward by remote control at night while he's asleep in his bed.'

'I can assure you, Sister, that *I'm* not prepared to hand over the postnatal management to a paediatrician,' asserted Rose.

'Look, Doctor, how may of you actually visit the postnatal ward during the night and see the problems at first hand?' countered Angela, her sharp, button-like eyes flashing.

Rose longed to return to her bed, but felt that this was a challenge she must accept. Besides, it would give more substance to her argument if she was armed with an on-the-spot account to report to Mr Horsfield.

Even so, she was quite unprepared for the tearful chaos that reigned throughout the postnatal ward. Before she reached the foot of the stairs the sound of crying babies and women's upraised voices seemed to come from all directions, and in particular from the four-bedded ward where Mrs Gainsford was literally shouting at Night Sister Hicks while Mrs Mowbray and the other two mothers listened open-mouthed.

'I'm telling you I'm not staying in this place one

minute longer! I've telephoned my husband to come to the hospital *now*, and take me home with our baby!' cried the frantic woman, her whole body shaking uncontrollably.

'The sooner the better, if you ask me,' muttered the young mother in the corner who was bottle-feeding her baby. 'We might all get a bit of peace!'

Jane Mowbray sighed, and exchanged a significant look with the other mother in the room.

Sister Doris Hicks was herself near to tears.

'*Please*, Mrs Gainsford, just try to keep calm and listen to reason, won't you?' she pleaded. 'Your baby is a big, hungry fellow who needs more milk than you've got at present, can't you *see*?'

Doris was a rather fussy, old-fashioned midwife, a widow in her fifties who worked part-time night duty to help support her son and daughter at college.

'I've looked after new babies for over thirty years,' she went on, 'and you can trust me to know what's best for your son — '

'That's just it, I *can't* trust you! You deliberately gave my son a bottle of that disgusting formula rubbish, against my wishes and against Dr Cranstone's instructions!' screamed the overwrought woman. 'Don't speak another *word* to me! I won't *listen* to you!'

Her voice rose on a hysterical shriek as Rose hurried into the four-bedder.

'All right, Mrs Gainsford, all right, there's no need to get so upset — you can leave here at any time, it isn't a prison,' Rose said with deliberate calm slowness, emphasising each word. 'All we ask is that you sign a form to say that you're discharging yourself and your baby.'

'I'll sign that I'm removing my child from that

woman's hands!' snapped Mrs Gainsford furiously. 'And Dr Cranstone will hear about this!'

'Oh, shut up, for God's sake!' exploded the house-wife and mother of three who also shared the four-bedder. 'Sister Hicks was only trying to get some food into that poor baby's empty stomach before he drove us all crazy!'

'That's right, Dr Gillis, I'm having nothing but trouble on nights these days!' sobbed Doris Hicks, the hairpins flying out of the untidy bun at the back of her greying head. 'Either they're complaining that they're being forced to breast-feed against their will, or else that their babies are being given bottle-feeds when they're supposed to be totally breast-fed. I can't stand it! I shall have to take early retirement, and then what will my poor Robert and Ruth do? They can't be expected to manage on their student grants!'

Rose suppressed a smile, and spoke firmly.

'Go into the office and sit down, Sister Hicks,' she ordered. 'And get somebody to put the kettle on for tea all round.' She knew that Doris had many years of experience, but not a great deal of emotional stamina. When the auxiliary nurse came in, Rose asked if there was a room where Mrs Gainsford could be alone with her baby.

'Chance'd be a fine thing,' replied the nurse gloom-ily. 'Two empty beds in yon ten-bedder, and everybody awake in there after all this hullaballoo. She'd best sit in t' treatment room while she waits for her husband.'

This particular auxiliary had worked nights on Post-natal for as long as anybody could remember, and had no hesitation in giving Rose the benefit of her opinion.

'Bloody daft carry-on,' she grumbled. 'If Dr Cranstone wants to run t'place according to his crack-

pot ideas, happen he'd better come over and give us a
hand for a few nights. *That'd* cure him!'

Rose listened to the sound of weary mothers trying to
soothe fretful babies in the heat of the summer night,
and by the time a bewildered Mr Gainsford had arrived
in response to his wife's sudden phone-call, she had
definitely decided to make no attempt to dissuade them
from going home with the baby. She was frankly worried
by a wildness in the wife's eyes, and felt that there was a
real possibility of psychiatric illness if she was subjected
to further stress. She spoke in an easy, friendly manner
to the couple, witnessing their signatures on the self-
discharge form, and accompanying them out to their car,
carrying the still crying baby which she handed carefully
to Mrs Gainsford in the back seat.

Returning to the ward office, she wrote a detailed
account of the incident in the patient's case-notes, and
asked for urgent letters to be sent to the GP and
community midwife, requesting early visits from them
both.

'Don't worry, Sister, I'll take full responsibility for
letting her go,' she told a worried Angela Grierson
who as acting nursing officer was accountable to the
senior midwife for all untoward events in the department. 'I totally support Sister Hicks in a very difficult
situation, but the postnatal policy on infant feeding and
management will have to be urgently reviewed. I'll
bring it to Mr Horsfield's attention today.'

Angela Grierson's button eyes darkened. 'It's the
midwives who'll be caught in the crossfire if there's a
row between the obs and the paeds,' she remarked
pessimistically.

Rose frowned. 'Look, Sister, I'm entirely on the side
of the midwives, and I have a little influence with Mr

Horsfield. He'll see things our way, he's a practical man.'

'I hope you're right, Dr Gillis. He's going to be furious about Mrs Gainsford,' rejoined the night sister.

'She'll be better off at home,' said Rose, glancing at her watch. It was nearly half-past three, and in spite of her tiredness she felt that she now truly understood the midwives' resentment of Dr Cranstone's too-rigid policy, and she did not begrudge the time she had spent talking with the postnatal patients and staff.

She was glad to hear the good news that a student midwife had just delivered the lady who had so dreaded having an induction of labour; everything had gone smoothly and quickly, with no other pain relief than a whiff of gas for the actual birth. Rose congratulated the new mother and her husband, and returned to her bed, though she tossed and turned, unable to get back to sleep. At seven she showered and dressed, and went down to the mess for breakfast.

'Rose, my love, how was your night on call? Is it all right if Phil and I join you?' asked Leigh McDowie, deftly balancing a tray with two bowls of muesli and a couple of poached eggs on toast. He was smiling down at her in undisguised delight, and she rather shyly returned his look, though the presence of Philip Cranstone was much less welcome to her.

'Please do.' The two doctors sat down beside her at the table for four. 'Are you both having coffee?' she asked, holding up the silver metal pot.

'Yes, please, Rose—thanks!' Leigh's voice held a hint of secret intimacy beneath the friendly manner he adopted in front of the paediatrician. 'Phil here has been up half the night on Kids with two quite nasty accidents, so-called. One's almost certainly a case of abuse, a poor little chap of three. We seem to get more of these incidents in hot weather, don't we, Phil?'

'Statistically, yes,' agreed the handsome, fair-haired man gravely, 'though of course the underlying causes are there all the time — the increase in the number of one-parent families, unemployment, poverty, general breakdown of family relationships. It's no good just throwing up our hands in horror, we've got to try to treat the whole situation of the family, starting with mother-and-baby interaction from the moment of birth.'

'I can see what you're getting at, Phil,' agreed Leigh, pouring milk on his muesli. 'This is the reason for the bee in your bonnet over rooming-in of babies with the mums, right?'

'Right. We need to aim for close early bonding — and what could be closer than breast-feeding? It makes sense for every reason,' replied Philip Cranstone.

Rose was sure that Leigh was deliberately encouraging Dr Cranstone to talk about his special subject for her benefit, and she realised that if she had been a young medical student listening to him in a lecture hall, she would be totally convinced by his arguments. Only she was no longer an impressionable student, but an experienced obstetric house officer with recent close contact with many new mothers; consequently she had some insight into their very different reactions to the experience of giving birth, and their differing social circumstances. And she was tired, just as a new mother was tired, and therefore emotionally vulnerable. She sipped her coffee slowly and thoughtfully.

'Haven't you got any comment, Rose?' Leigh asked her pleasantly. 'You can see what Phil's aiming for, can't you? I know you haven't been too happy lately about the postnatal policy, but don't you see that it's something we've got to take on board, and make it work?'

Rose put down her cup.

'I can appreciate your motives, Dr Cranstone,' she said, choosing each word carefully. 'It's just that I think you're going about it in the wrong way. Firstly, you haven't enough flexibility in your attitude towards the mothers and their differences as individuals — and every baby is different, too. Secondly, you haven't consulted the midwives and learned from their experience. Sister Hicks, for example, is old enough to be your mother, and was looking after mothers and babies before you were born — she's nearly at her wits' end because of your splendid theories. *I* spent some time up last night, too, in Postnatal, and I don't know how anybody can be expected to get any rest in that place. The noise and the tension is unbelievable, and I'm particularly worried about one patient who took her own discharge at three o'clock this morning. You remember Mrs Gainsford, don't you, Leigh?'

'Mrs Gainsford?' echoed Leigh, dropping his spoon. 'That intelligent schoolteacher who was having a bit of a struggle to breast-feed? My God, Rose! Whatever happened?'

'She's a highly-strung woman who's managed to organise her life succesfully up to now,' replied Rose sharply. 'But since the trauma of childbirth and the hormonal imbalance it causes, plus the fact that her lactation is just not sufficient for a large, hungry baby with a very loud voice, she's flipped her lid. So I let her go without any argument, because I considered it to be the lesser evil.'

'But there must have been something that triggered

it off, surely?' questioned Leigh, his dark eyes probing hers.

'Yes. Sister Hicks quietened the baby with a formula feed, and——'

'But she'd no right to give a bottle-feed without permission!' objected Philip.

'Just tell me what else she should have done!' retorted Rose impatiently. 'And I'll tell *you* something, Dr Cranstone. That woman's heading for a postnatal psychosis unless her GP and community midwife have got more sense—and sensitivity—than she's been shown here. Her baby's starving, and needs some *milk*, for God's sake!'

'But her lactation will improve,' began Leigh.

'Not in her present state of mind, it won't,' snapped Rose. 'Nothing dries up the supply more quickly than emotional upset. That baby will end up bottle-fed, and the mother's going to feel a total failure.'

'But Annette hasn't had all this hassle over a perfectly normal function,' remonstrated Philip, not noticing Leigh's warning glance.

Rose's dark blue eyes blazed.

'If you think that every woman should be like your wife, I've got news for you! Every woman is different! Mothers with sore tails, Caesarean incisions, afterpains, cracked nipples—they can't cope with a ward full of howling babies round the clock, it's sheer *hell*, even the good breast-feeders are upset by the atmosphere. I'm going to speak to Mr Horsfield about it today.'

Philip Cranstone drew a long breath, obviously preparing to be patient with a difficult young woman.

'I agree that perhaps there should have been more consultation with the midwives,' he conceded with a smile. 'Some of them may find it a little hard to accept, but if they can only get rid of their prejudices and work with me instead of against me, I aim to achieve my target of total rooming-in and ninety per cent breast-feeding within the next three months.'

He sat back, clearly expecting a more positive response from Rose. Leigh held his breath, waiting for her to explode. Neither of them was prepared for her icy contempt.

'I realise that you're young and well-meaning, Dr Cranstone, but you lack practical experience in maternity work, especially the psychological aspect of it. The midwives could teach you a great deal if you weren't so arrogant——'

'Just a moment, Dr Gillis!' exclaimed Philip Cranstone, flushing angrily.

Rose raised her voice. 'I warn you, I shall do everything I can to stop you upsetting my postnatal patients and antagonising perfectly reasonable staff. If you gentlemen will excuse me, I'll take my breakfast to another table.'

As she got up from her chair and piled her cup, saucer and plate on to a tray, Leigh finally lost his patience with her.

'Rose, for heaven's sake! Damn it all, Phil is a paediatric registrar!'

'Big deal. And I'm a woman,' she returned.

'And may I ask if you've ever breast-fed a baby, Dr Gillis?'

'Not yet, Dr McDowie. Have *you*?' It was a declaration of war.

# CHAPTER FIVE

AFTER the ward-round Mr Horsfield and his team were seated in the upstairs office with a tray of coffee. The fragrant aroma of this and the consultant's fine Havana cigar drifted down the corridor as he began his customary discussion, beginning by complimenting Leigh McDowie on his astute guess at Trish Pendle's kidney condition, and asking the two students Ben and Dan for their ideas on how she should be delivered, and how soon.

Rose prayed that he would not ask her any questions, as she was bracing herself for the subject of postnatal management. Mr Horsfield had told her that he would bring up this issue after he had talked about the other problems — Trish Pendle and Mrs Edna Lambert who had now reached thirty-seven weeks with a low-lying placenta that could start separating at any time and cause a sudden haemorrhage. Knowing her agitation, the consultant tactfully left her out of the question-and-answer session with the students; he approved Leigh's suggestion that the surgical team should be asked to see Trish and advise before deciding on an early Caesarean section.

Rose usually found these informal discussions highly entertaining, and admired the consultant's cunning skill as a teacher, phrasing his questions as if he were asking for advice. The medical students would never forget Trish and what they had learned from her tragic situation. This morning, however, Rose was rigidly tense, looking straight ahead, pale and unsmiling with dark circles of fatigue beneath her eyes. At one point she glanced at Leigh, to find him gazing at her intently, his eyes full of concern. She hastily looked away, though her heart sank. Just at this time in her life when she needed every ounce of vitality to cope with the demands of her mother's terminal illness and also hold down a responsible job, she now had to do battle with a highly respected paediatrician. She would have been so glad of Leigh's support, but knew that he agreed in principle with Dr Cranstone. As for Paul, she suspected that he would have little sympathy with a problem that was not his concern.

'Right, I think we've covered our antenatals,' said Mr Horsfield, putting down his cup and stubbing his cigar in the ashtray. Rose stiffened as she lifted up her chin defiantly. This was it.

'We now come to the postnatal ward, where things are not as they should be,' Mr Horsfield continued. 'Unfortunately a patient saw fit to discharge herself in the early hours of this morning, and this incident has led Dr Gillis to call for an urgent review of the postnatal policy. As you know, Dr Philip Cranstone, the senior paediatric registrar, is deputising for Dr Cameron, who's in Ethiopia, and finding life very distressing indeed out there. Hundreds of children are starving and dying of gastro-enteritis and other unpleasant diseases. I think we should get our own problems into perspective and bear in mind how fortunate our mothers and babies at Beltonshaw General are by comparison with that terrible situation, whatever we may feel about our policies here. Agreed?'

There were nods and sounds of assent from the team, all intent on his words.

'I had more or less decided to give Dr Cranstone a free hand, during his consultant's absence, to put his well-known beliefs into practice in our postnatal ward, and to keep a low profile myself,' he went on. 'You must all know that Dr Cranstone advocates rooming-in of babies with their mothers at all times during the day and night, and a strong emphasis on breast-feeding. Rooming-in has of course become popular, though there is a great deal of local variation. So what has Dr Gillis to say to us?'

He nodded towards Rose, who drew a deep breath and proceeded to speak with a vehemence that none of them had expected.

'As I've already told you, Mr Horsfield, I spent some time in the postnatal ward last night, and was present when Mrs Gainsford took her own discharge with her baby. I was appalled by the unhappy atmosphere of the whole ward, the dissatisfaction of the mothers and midwives alike — and I simply cannot believe that you intend to allow Dr Cranstone to go on using our patients as guinea-pigs to try out his ridiculous theories——'

'My dear Dr Gillis, let's not make subjective judgements before we've examined all the facts,' interrupted Mr Horsfield with a slight frown. 'I'm giving you this opportunity to put your views to your colleagues on the obstetric team, but perhaps we should hear some other opinions first. McDowie, I believe you're a firm advocate of breast-feeding?'

'Certainly, sir, in principle,' replied Leigh at once, looking straight at the consultant. 'Obviously, if a woman honestly doesn't want to feed her child herself, then nobody can force her to do so, nor would this be advisable——'

'I should damned well think *not*!' exploded Rose, unable to contain herself. 'Though with men like Dr Cranstone and yourself putting subtle pressures on them, they're made to feel inadequate and uncaring if they decide to bottle-feed. And we obstetricians appear to be sitting back and letting our mothers wrestle with unworkable ideals at the whim of male theorists!'

'Dr Gillis, we're not going to get anywhere if we allow ourselves to be swept away by emotion,' reproved Mr Horsfield, not unkindly. 'Let's just hear Dr McDowie out, please.'

'I appreciate Dr Gillis's strong feelings and her frankness, sir,' said Leigh, addressing the consultant. 'But for certain personal reasons, for which we all deeply sympathise with her, she's been under a lot of stress lately, and perhaps not quite so able to make an unbiased judgement.'

'Mrs Gainsford has been under a lot of stress and wasn't able to make an unbiased judgement when she took herself off!' retorted Rose furiously. 'The woman was beside herself, absolutely at breaking point — I saw her myself, and — '

'Mrs Gainsford is an extreme case,' interrupted the consultant, raising his voice a little. 'I've been on the phone to her GP and he says she's at present under sedation at home. The grandmother is looking after the family, including that endlessly crying baby, who is now having bottle feeds and has quietened down at last, I'm thankful to hear.'

'Of course he has, now that he's being *fed*!' stormed Rose. 'And yet Sister Hicks was blamed and verbally abused for doing just that!'

Leigh McDowie took a breath, and spoke to Rose as gently as he could. 'Point taken, Dr Gillis, but perhaps

Sister Hicks was just a little bit tactless in her approach to Mrs Gainsford. She's a good soul in her way, of course, but ——'

'How dare you?' Rose spat out the words. 'How *dare* you speak in that patronising way about a conscientious midwife? Doris Hicks knows her duty towards *all* her patients, babies as well as mothers — and Dr Cranstone owes her an apology for all the aggravation she's been caused. At least she lives in the real world, which is more than can be said for him or for you — condescending idiots!'

She almost choked, and tears sprang to her eyes; she blinked them away fiercely. There was a general gasp from the company, and Leigh's mouth was grimly set. Mr Horsfield took off his spectacles and rubbed the lenses as he considered his next words. He was soon to go on his annual holiday in the Algarve, and had no wish to precipitate the resignation of a good senior house officer before his departure.

'You've stated your case forcefully, and left us in no doubt of your convictions, Dr Gillis,' he said carefully. 'I know your strong words are prompted by a genuine concern for our postnatal mothers and their babies.'

'Thank you for *that* much, at least, sir,' she responded, 'but I have to tell you that I'm not prepared to go on seeing them distressed and upset at a difficult time of readjustment in their lives. It's nothing short of disgraceful, and will earn our maternity department a bad name for its postnatal treatment — and deservedly so!'

'Thank you, Doctor,' said the consultant with deliberate politeness. 'Now, I want the close attention of you all, as I've made a decision that I hope will be acceptable.'

He looked hard at Rose, who stared straight back at him.

'I'll give Dr Cranstone's experimental policy another six weeks, until I return from my leave — that brings us to mid-September. During this period Dr Gillis has my personal authority to overrule the policy in any individual case where she feels that the best interests of the mother or baby — or both — are not being served. I wonder if Dr Gillis might care to undertake a research survey of the policy which she could present to both the obstetric and paediatric teams at the end of the period. Does that sound fair to you, Dr Gillis? You realise that I'm relying very heavily on your judgement and common sense, especially during my absence?'

Two red spots of colour had appeared on Rose's white cheeks, but her voice was steady as she replied.

'Yes, sir, I understand, and I'll certainly carry out a survey.'

'And what about you, Dr McDowie?' asked the consultant, suddenly focusing on Leigh. 'Are you prepared to assist Dr Gillis with this survey?'

Leigh's face was expressionless as he gave his considered reply.

'No, sir, I'm afraid not. While I have the deepest respect for Dr Gillis's sincerity ——'

'Which means that he totally opposes me,' cut in Rose angrily.

Leigh did not look in her direction, but raised his voice a little.

'I must ask Dr Gillis to show me the same respect, and allow me to answer your question, sir,' he said evenly.

Mr Horsfield looked meaningly towards Rose, and held up a hand commanding her silence.

'As I said, while taking account of Dr Gillis's entrenched position on this matter, I feel that to oppose a policy which is becoming accepted nationally is rather like swimming against the tide, isn't it?'

'I understand what you're saying, Dr McDowie, but will you answer my question?' Mr Horsfield persisted. 'Are you prepared to assist Dr Gillis with this survey?'

'No, sir. I don't see how I can, given our completely opposing views.' Leigh spoke with cold finality.

'That's no surprise to me,' declared Rose bitterly. 'I'm perfectly prepared to fight a rearguard action single-handed on behalf of our mothers and babies.'

'If, as you say, the *midwives* are on your side, you're not exactly single-handed, Doctor,' remarked the consultant slyly. 'A most formidable force behind you, I'd say!'

'And *I'd* like to back Dr Gillis, sir, all the way,' broke in Ben, red-faced but emphatic. 'As she is a woman in a woman's field, sir, I bow to her greater knowledge of women, sir,' he ended in some confusion.

'Well said, young man, well said!' Mr Horsfield told him, suppressing a smile. 'Are there any further comments on this subject before lunch?'

'I'd like to put a question to you, sir,' said Rose. 'May I ask what is the policy at St Agnes's Maternity Home? I believe you send some of your private patients there.' Her face was expressionless.

'Yes, I do, Doctor. Well, every mother has a single room at St Agnes's, so the question of rooming-in is easier there. As regards feeding—yes, the mothers do have a choice as to how their babies are fed.'

'I thought as much, sir. You can't very well force crackpot theories on to patients who are paying a considerable amount of money, can you?'

They all held their breath as they waited for his reply. Mr Horsfield was not a man to swallow a gibe, not even from a favourite house officer. His eyes glinted behind his gold half-moons.

'Let me tell you something I very rarely talk about, Dr Gillis. My own daughter had a very difficult labour, under the care of an eminent obstetrician at a university hospital,' he said evenly. 'After a huge episiotomy and a failed forceps delivery, she was rushed into the theatre for an emergency Caesarean section. She was quite poorly for the next few days, and in a great deal of discomfort. However, my daughter had made up her mind to breast-feed my granddaughter, and succeeded in doing so, for six months. And I can certify that she was not subjected to anybody's crackpot ideas. Any comments?'

'Yes, sir, you've shown the importance of motivation,' answered Rose quietly. 'A woman who's determined to breast-feed can sometimes succeed against heavy odds, whereas another will use any excuse to give up as soon as possible. All women are different, that's my point, and shouldn't be treated as clones. And may I congratulate you on having a very brave daughter!'

Mr Horsfield beamed upon them all as he dismissed the meeting, asking Rose to stay behind for a few minutes.

Leigh touched her arm as he went out, and tried to whisper something to her, but she totally ignored him, and he strode away to the canteen, where he sat and ate his lunch alone, silently cursing the issue that had caused the rift between them. Presently the lively conversation of the nurses at a nearby table intruded on his thoughts; they were from Female Surgical, and were giggling over Dr Sykes's preoccupation with Caroline Trench.

Leigh experienced a wave of angry impatience with Rose that had nothing whatever to do with the postnatal policy. . .

'Now, what about your mother, my dear?' asked Mr Horsfield. 'She tells me her sister is coming over from Ireland to lend a hand.'

'That's right, sir,' smiled Rose. 'My aunt Maura's arriving on Thursday, so I hope to take my mother home on Friday, if that's OK with you.'

'Good! And it's your weekend off, so make the most of it, Rose. The summer's passing, and this sunshine won't last for much longer, you know.' His voice was grave, and there was a deeper meaning to his words.

Rose at once set about planning her survey. In addition to her normally long hours she began a daily round of the postnatal ward, speaking to every patient and recording her comments, and also questioning the staff on duty. At least one night in three saw her spending up to an hour in the ward after midnight, talking to the midwives and auxiliaries on duty, and any patient who was awake. She engaged the services of Mr Horsfield's secretary Miss Kavanagh, and drew up two questionnaires, one to be presented to each patient on arrival in Postnatal with her baby, and one to be completed just before discharge home. Miss Kavanagh agreed to assist Rose in compiling a dossier from all these sources of information, to be presented to Mr Horsfield and Dr Cranstone at the end of six weeks. The postnatal staff were delighted by her fierce determination, and gave her all the co-operation she needed; Dr Rose was on the warpath!

The pressures began to mount, however, and the strain showed in tension lines around her eyes, a droop at the corners of her mouth, and the lifelessness of her usually glossy hair, pulled relentlessly back into a twisted coil and pinned in place. She was far from happy, and this was not only because of the postnatal policy, or even the sadness of her mother's illness. Try as she would, she could not get Leigh McDowie out of her thoughts, and the deep disappointment over what she saw as his failure to support her. She knew his good qualities and caring attitude towards the patients, especially those with medical and social problems. It seemed so regrettable, so *silly* for them to be on opposite sides of a dispute which soon reverberated through the whole hospital; in fact it was becoming almost a joke that a self-opinionated female house officer and a group of diehard midwives were actually defying Philip Cranstone's splendid policy of promoting closer bonding between mothers and their babies.

Paul Sykes expressed this viewpoint forcibly. 'For heaven's sake, darling, you've got enough on your plate right now, without trying to outwit Phil Cranstone! He'll get his way in the end, so why waste your energy?'

'Thanks for your support, Paul,' Rose returned.

He shrugged. 'Oh, well, if you're not prepared to see reason, there's no point in talking. Do you know that they're calling you the Ombudswoman?'

'I'm flattered. Oh, Paul, by the way, Mother's being discharged on Friday. Could you possibly — I mean, I just wondered if you'll be able to drive her home?'

'Sorry, darling, but Friday's out. Caroline's having her plaster changed and her leg X-rayed,' he apologised. 'Keep your fingers crossed that it won't need doing again! Er—why don't you just ring for a taxi when your mother's ready to leave Gynae?'

'Well, yes, of course I can.' Rose felt a little chilled, and not for the first time she began to question the depth of Paul's attachment to her. It had started as such a perfect love affair following their encounter at the Hallowe'en party, and she had committed herself to him with such complete trust: he was the only man who had possessed her body, and he had told her that she was the only woman who had ever truly possessed his heart and mind. Now the thought suddenly came into her head that they might never spend another weekend in the caravan at Nethersedge, and this gave her a curious mixture of emotions, a sense almost of relief combined with a shiver of loneliness. Without Paul—and without her mother—she felt that she would be very much alone—the *Ombudswoman*!

For Rose was totally unaware that Leigh McDowie watched her constantly, noting all the signs of strain and fatigue. Like her, he secretly cursed the ill-timed dispute over postnatal policy, and even though he felt morally bound to support Dr Cranstone in public, he did what he could to ease Rose's burden, diplomatically steering her away to the antenatal ward or delivery unit when Dr Cranstone did his rounds on Postnatal. In the doctors' mess he kept a free place for her at the corner table where she liked to sit alone, eating her hasty meals behind her favourite newspaper which magically appeared daily on her chair, apparently casually discarded. . .

And when she went to see her mother in the gynae ward on Thursday, Leigh was already there beside the bed.

'Will ye listen to this man, Rose? He says he'll meet Maura off the boat at Liverpool, so he will!'

Rose hardly knew how to meet his eye, but he tried to put her at ease by requesting a favour in return.

'You'll cover for me, won't you, Rose, if I shoot off a bit early this afternoon? I'll deliver Auntie to your home, then whizz back here to take over your bleep, so you can go and say your hundred thousand welcomes to her!'

'I just don't know what to say,' faltered Rose, suddenly conscious of her tired face, crumpled white coat and hair badly in need of a shampoo. 'Aunt Maura said she'll take the train, but it would be so nice for her to be met. How will you know her?'

'Sure, he'll hold up a piece o' paper sayin', "Miss Maura Carlinnagh, I've come to meet ye"! She'll see him as soon as she steps off!' enthused Brigid, her thin face alight with happiness at the thought of seeing her sister again. 'Oh, Rose, isn't he the *lovely* man?'

Again, Rose could not meet his teasing eyes. 'It's just so terribly good of you, Leigh, and of course I'll cover for you as soon as you want to get away. There's only one patient in labour right now, poor Mrs Taylor.'

'Yes, that dear soul who's had God knows how many prostin suppositories, and still didn't get her induction till this morning,' nodded Leigh. 'Do you think she'll make it for her mum's fiftieth birthday do on Sunday?'

'Not if she ends up with a section,' sighed Rose. 'She'd have to stay in for at least a week afterwards, wouldn't she?'

'Yeah — and I think David Rowan probably *will* chop her before the day's out if she doesn't dilate up,' Leigh predicted.

'Mother o' Heaven, what do ye mean?' asked Brigid, aghast.

'A Caesarean, Mother—don't look so worried!' smiled Rose. 'Look, Leigh, I'll pop up to the delivery unit now and see how she is. Maybe if we accelerate the syntocinon drip and top up the epidural, the cervix might decide to dilate, and we could get away with a forceps or a Vantouse extraction.'

'You see how my lady boss has got it all worked out?' said Leigh, winking at Brigid.

'I never had an idea o' how clever she is, that girl o' mine,' marvelled Brigid. 'I'm very glad I've found out—oh, and before ye go to that poor soul, Rose, Leigh says he'll take me home tomorrow as soon as I'm ready. Sure, I told him I'd be off first thing in the mornin', but he says I'll have to wait for his coffee break!'

Rose could only convey her thanks with a grateful look, comparing his voluntary offer to Paul's negative response to her request.

When Leigh returned from meeting Maura Carlinnagh and bringing her straight to the gynae ward to be united with her sister, he hurried up the stairs to the delivery unit, where he was greeted by three triumphant ladies: Rose Gillis and Sister Pardoe with an exhausted but overjoyed Mrs Taylor holding her new baby boy.

'Well done! How did you manage it?' he grinned, sharing their delight at the final outcome of a very long wait.

'Dr Rose said I could do it, and I *did*!' declared the new mother proudly. 'It took me nearly two hours to push him out, but there he is! Isn't he *gorgeous*?'

'I thought I was going to have to put Wrigley's

forceps on, but as soon as I did the episiotomy, he came of his own accord!' whispered Rose to Leigh as they all admired the chubby new arrival.

'Now, Mrs Taylor, are you going to breast-feed?' asked Sister Pardoe. Rose and Leigh avoided each other's eyes.

'Of course I am! Come on, my precious boy, come to your mummy,' cooed the doting newly delivered mother to her child, who immediately attached himself to the soft ample breast she offered him, and proved to be a naturally good feeder from the start.

They presented a beautiful picture, and Leigh stared at Rose as she bent over the delivery bed, her sterile green gown falling off one shoulder and revealing a glimpse of the sweet, warm division showing above a lacy white bra.

And he allowed himself to imagine her in his arms, with all that beauty revealed to his hands and lips. As if feeling his gaze, she suddenly turned and caught the look in his eyes. Her pale cheeks flushed, and she immediately pulled the shapeless green gown up over her shoulder.

And they were both aware of the invisible current that had passed between them. Rose was startled by the frank admiration — and more than admiration — in Leigh's dark, expressive eyes, and it gave her a curious sense of reassurance. She was reminded that she was still an attractive woman who could arouse desire in a male colleague, even one who was firmly opposed to her standpoint.

The recollection of his look stayed in her memory, and could not be easily dismissed. . .

# CHAPTER SIX

MAURA CARLINNAGH was scarcely able to hide her emotion when she saw her elder sister's changed appearance, and the two of them clung together silently on their first meeting. When Maura found her voice, she began to scold.

'Sure, Bridie, none of us iver understood why ye upped and left us to marry that feller that none of your family iver saw! Why didn't ye bring him home to see us, Bridie, girl?' she asked, smoothing back her sister's white hair and gazing reproachfully into the faded blue eyes. Brigid had been the cleverest of the Carlinnaghs, held in awe by her younger brothers and sisters, especially when she went to the training college and then returned to her home village to become a respected teacher at the school they had all attended as children.

As Maura embraced Brigid's thin frame, she came to an immediate decision.

'They'll have to manage widout me at home for a while, so they will. I'm goin' to look after ye, sister, and stay wid ye until — until ye're better and can do widout me,' she promised in a hasty torrent of words that ended in a sob.

The bustling Irish spinster was as good as her word, and Rose was filled with relief and gratitude towards the aunt she scarcely knew. Maura on her part was open-mouthed in admiration at the sight of the efficient, attractive young woman doctor.

'Heaven have mercy, Rose! How have ye kept goin', working' all the hours God made, and tryin' to look after your mother an' all! Why didn't ye write before, Rose? How could ye let me sister face such an operation widout lettin' her family know? But niver mind, I'm here now, and here I'm goin' to stay!'

From then on much of Rose's burden was lifted, and it was a joy to her to see the reunited sisters together, constantly joking and reminiscing about old times as Maura organised the household around the invalid's needs. Cushions were arranged on the sofa in the front parlour, and small but tasty meals were brought on trays. A comfortable padded garden chair with a leg-rest was delivered to the house, and lying on it, Brigid drowsed away the summer afternoons in comfort.

'It arrived out o' the blue, Rose, wid a card that just said, "From a devoted admirer",' explained Maura. 'Now have ye any idea who could have sent it to her?'

Rose *had*, and was touched when Leigh McDowie popped in to pay Brigid an occasional visit; they would sit together in the little back garden, while Maura brought tea and freshly baked scones arranged on a small wicker table. Looking back later, Rose was always to remember those golden afternoons as the August days went by, still very warm, though misty mornings and darkening evenings warned that autumn was drawing closer.

Life in the maternity department went on; Paul Sykes's examination of Trish Pendle brought him to the conclusion that she should be speedily delivered and then subjected to a battery of kidney function tests before deciding on major surgery for her non-functioning left kidney. An elective Caesarean section produced a small but healthy baby boy, and Trish called him Donovan. Mrs McClennan the social worker arranged for him to go to a foster-mother when Trish was transferred to Female Surgical.

'My God, Rose, what a *lump* that Pendle girl is!' groaned Paul over lunch in the doctors' mess. 'I ask you, what can be done with creatures like that? Overweight, unintelligent, and adding to Beltonshaw's housing problems by producing a kid that she can't look after! There's something to be said for compulsory sterilisation in cases like that — I know you won't agree with me, but that's my gut reaction.'

Rose could not help remembering Leigh McDowie's sympathy for the unfortunate teenager and her baby; she felt that Paul's remark was not deserving of an answer.

'Have you received your invitation to Caroline's farewell party?' he asked, and Rose nodded without enthusiasm. The shattered bones of the actress's leg had set together very well, a triumph for Paul's careful manipulation; a new plaster had been applied, and Caroline was now able to walk around the ward on crutches. She was delighted at the prospect of going home, and had obtained permission from the Health Authority to throw a party in the hospital boardroom on the evening before her discharge. She had invited all the hospital staff who had aided her recovery, with their friends and partners, and Paul was to be guest of honour. As members of the medical team who had assisted in A and E on the day of the M63 accident, Leigh and Rose were invited, and Rose heard Tanya Dickenson telling Laurie Moffatt that he had asked her to go as his partner; she had noted the satisfaction in the midwife's cool blue eyes.

Meanwhile Rose's determination to keep up the

battle on behalf of the postnatal mothers and their babies continued unabated, though she had never in her life felt so tired. Junior doctors' hours were long enough without the addition of daily and nightly research; the demands of her self-imposed task took their toll, and she lost weight. The only times that she relaxed were during the snatched hours spent at home with her mother and Aunt Maura, and by the third week in August, Rose realised that she was thoroughly run down; nevertheless she forced herself to go on devoting the same amount of time to her survey, conferring regularly with Miss Kavanagh as the growing pile of information was fed into the computer in the medical secretary's office.

When a heavy and painful period started, Rose skipped lunch while she rested on her bed in the residency before the afternoon's operation list, which included Mrs Lambert's Caesarean section. A little girl was safely extracted by Mr Rowan with Rose assisting, and the list continued with gynaecological operations. As the time crept on to four o'clock, Rose suddenly felt the theatre darkening around her, as if a network of grey threads was obscuring her vision. She shook her head, but the threads became thicker and blacker until they completely blotted out the light. The floor of the theatre swirled round giddily, and far away she heard David Rowan's voice calling out, 'She's falling! Somebody catch hold of her, for heaven's sake!'

And then she was lying shivering on the smooth, cold tiled floor, a burly theatre technician was supporting her head, and a student nurse was holding a glass of iced water to her lips.

'She's coming round,' said a disembodied voice.

'It's all right, Dr Gillis, you've just had a little faint,' said the technician. 'Here, give me your arms and I'll take you out of here.'

She put limp arms around his neck and felt herself lifted bodily and carried through the door. He laid her on a trolley in the recovery annexe.

'This is all so silly,' she whispered between white lips. 'Mr Rowan can't operate alone.'

'Yes, he can. There are only a couple of D and Cs left to do now, and the theatre sister can cope,' said the staff nurse on duty in Recovery. 'Dr Rowan has asked me to telephone for a taxi to take you home for the rest of the day. Frankly, Dr Gillis, you look shattered. Go straight to bed when you get home, and have a good rest.'

Rose felt that she could indeed sleep for a week, and the staff nurse assisted her to change out of theatre greens and put on her summer dress and sandals. She was escorted to the hospital entrance, where she sank thankfully into the back seat of the taxi and closed her eyes.

'Mother o' heaven, whatever's the matter?' asked Aunt Maura in alarm when Rose walked in through the back door.

'It's all right, Auntie, I—I've been given the rest of the day off,' answered Rose as brightly as she could. 'Where's Mother?'

Maura lowered her voice and pointed to the closed door of the little front room that was always called the parlour.

'Ssh, Rose, she's in there conferrin',' she whispered. 'And not to be disturbed on any account,' she added solemnly.

'Conferring? Who's she conferring with?' demanded Rose. 'Has Father Naylor called?'

'No, he's — er —' faltered Maura in confusion, and Rose became suspicious. If their GP Dr Tait was with her mother, or if Brigid had asked to see a solicitor, Rose felt that she had a right to know, if not actually to be present. She moved towards the parlour door, and could just hear the murmur of her mother's voice, though not clearly enough to listen to the words.

Then came the voice of Leigh McDowie, gentle and deep, and the unmistakable word 'Rose', followed by something she could not quite catch, and again the word 'Rose'.

With an angry exclamation, 'What on earth — !' Rose opened the door and stood looking down at the pair of them as they sat together at the table on which a number of documents were spread out.

'What's going on here?' she asked with an annoyance that sprang from anxiety and fatigue. 'What are you doing here, Dr McDowie? What right have you to come here in my absence and discuss me with my own mother? What's *this*?' she added, stepping forward to seize an official-looking certificate from the table. Leigh quickly forestalled her, covering it with his hand.

'Not so fast, Rose. Your mother and I have every right to hold a private discussion if she so wishes. We weren't expecting you —'

'Obviously not!' she retorted, her face white with fury as her voice rose higher. 'I'm only her daughter, after all! Oh, what *is* it between you two, the way you plot and scheme together, as thick as thieves? What is this *conspiracy* against me? Mother, I demand to be told what you've been saying to this man!'

'No, Rose, *no*!' Brigid almost shrieked, covering her face with her hands. Rose stared in horror, and Leigh put his arm around Brigid, drawing her head against his shoulder and whispering gentle reassurances into her ear. He then looked up at Rose with quiet but unanswerable authority.

'Kindly leave us, Rose,' he ordered. 'And close the door behind you, please.'

Aghast, Rose did as she was told, and collapsed into the arms of a distraught Maura, who led her into the kitchen where she sank down on to a chair.

'Sure and there's no harm in the man, Rose,' soothed her aunt. 'She *sent* for him, so she did, and I wasn't to be tellin' ye—but Brigid would *niver* plot against ye, Rose, ye must know that.'

'I know, I know—oh, poor Mother, whatever's troubling her?' sobbed the exhausted young woman. She wiped her eyes hastily when Leigh appeared. He looked at her steadily, and spoke in a calm and quiet way.

'You're to promise me never to mention this business to your mother, Rose, my dear. She's suffered quite enough. Maura, is the kettle on? You could do with a good strong Irish brew all round, and Brigid is to rest.'

He turned to Rose and took hold of her hand.

'Have I your promise?' he insisted.

She nodded and whispered, 'Yes.'

'Good girl. Now, what have you been up to? You look like a little ghost. Did you faint in Theatre or something?'

She forced a smile. 'That's exactly right, I'm afraid,' she muttered, and Maura fussed over her, lifting her legs up on to another chair and tucking a cushion behind her back.

'Good heavens, woman, you'll kill yourself with overwork!' cried Leigh in concern. 'Go to bed, and stay there till morning—I'll cover for you tonight.'

'No, I'm due to visit Postnatal after midnight for my research project,' Rose told him wearily.

'To hell with *that*!' he retorted.

'You don't know how important this is to me, Leigh. I'll have a rest now, but I *must* go in for my night visit, no matter what anybody says, yourself included.'

He made an effort to control his exasperation, but did not quite succeed.

'Look, Rose, *I'll* go in and do the bloody research on Postnatal! I'll take a notebook and clipboard and be the Ombudswoman for tonight—I'll chat them all up, I'll listen to everybody, I'll change nappies and plonk babies on to breasts, I'll make mad, passionate love to Sister Hicks in the patients' bath, I'll do *anything*, just so long as you'll stay here and have a proper night's sleep, for the lord's sake!'

'All right,' Rose capitulated suddenly, because she was truly afraid that she might collapse in uncontrollable, hysterical laughter if they continued to argue.

When Leigh marched out of the house after a few final private words with Brigid, Maura looked thoughtfully at her niece.

'Sure, it's plain to see that doctor cares about ye, Rose,' she said.


Rose collapsed into her bed before nine o'clock, and slept deeply and dreamlessly until woken by Aunt Maura with tea at seven the next morning. She felt wonderfully refreshed in body and mind as she reported at the hospital an hour later, and knew that she must thank Leigh for allowing her to enjoy such an untroubled rest. She did not get a chance to speak to him all the morning, as she was working in Maternity and he was in Gynae, but she looked out for him at lunchtime in the mess.

Philip Cranstone and his wife Annette were seated with the paediatric team at a table near to hers, and when she saw Leigh leaving the serving-hatch with his tray, she assumed that he would go and join them. To her surprise he waved an acknowledgement of Philip's, 'Over here, Leigh!' and then came over to her table where he put down his lunch of roast lamb and vegetables, fruit and coffee.

'All right if I join you, Rose? I'm sorry to intrude on your meal, but I'd like a word or three, if you don't mind.'

Rose was halfway through her usual salad; she folded up her newspaper and smiled hesitantly. She felt a little flustered, remembering the scene at her home the day before.

'Of course, Leigh, feel free. I was — er — hoping I'd see you, actually.'

'First of all, are you fit to be working today?' he enquired. 'You looked all in yesterday afternoon.'

'I'm fine, honestly, thanks to a really wonderful, uninterrupted night's sleep, and I'm really grateful to you, Leigh,' she continued hastily, lowering her eyes and cutting into the broccoli quiche on her plate. 'As a matter of fact, I owe you an apology. I shouldn't have burst in on you and my mother in the way that I did.'

'How is Brigid today?' he asked quickly.

'Fine. She was still asleep when I left this morning, and looked as if she'd had a peaceful night.'

Forcing herself to look straight at him, she saw that his eyes were shadowed and lacked their usual quirky humour.

'What sort of a night did *you* have, anyway?' she asked. 'Postnatal must have been quite busy, with Mrs

Lambert's Caesarean section and quite a few newly delivered ——'

She broke off and looked up to see Philip Cranstone standing beside them, beaming in his most charming manner.

'Hi, Leigh — and Rose, dear, how are you? Come on, both of you, and join us. Annette's longing to hear the latest tall stories from Maternity, and we might as well be sociable!'

Rose lowered her face and was silent; Leigh's response was unexpectedly offhand.

'Sorry, Phil, but I'm having a private talk right now, and not feeling quite in the mood to entertain the luncheon club today. Sorry.'

Philip raised his eyebrows, and returned to his table with a shrug.

'Listen, Rose, I want to share this research project with you,' said Leigh seriously. 'All right, so I know I said I wouldn't join in, but now I honestly think that it needs at least two researchers. There's no reason why we can't tackle the work together, even if we are on opposite sides of the argument. Actually it would give a better balance to the survey.'

Rose searched his face, suspecting an ulterior motive. She had no wish to have her findings diluted or falsely interpreted.

'Do you mean that you've changed your mind about Dr Cranstone's policy?' she asked him bluntly.

'Let's just say that I'm as eager as you are to produce firm, documented evidence to shove in front of the bigwigs,' he replied. 'And you *can't* go on doing all this slogging on your own, Rose — from now on I'm going to do my share, unless one of us drops dead before it's finished,' he added under his breath.

'I must admit that it's been getting me down a bit lately,' she admitted reluctantly.

'That's obvious. You've worn yourself out, Rose, but help is now available, I promise. And after all this hassle, I want to see the results published in the medical and nursing press. The national dailies and women's magazines could well pick it up and give the whole issue a wider airing—not a bad idea. Only we *have* to get our facts and figures right—no anecdotal stuff!'

Rose put down her knife and fork and turned her deep-blue eyes full on her erstwhile opponent, quite unaware of the effect this had on him.

'Tell me, Leigh, what particular aspect of your experience last night brought about this eagerness to take part in my survey?'

He shook his head. 'Don't jump to conclusions, Rose. I'm not about to change sides after just a couple of hours on one fairly hectic night,' he said guardedly. 'It's important to keep emotions out of this sort of investigation. It only covers six weeks, and will only include about a hundred and fifty mothers, if that. Are you happy for me to be in on it?'

Rose sighed and slowly nodded. 'As long as we have access to each other's data at any time, Leigh, and let Miss Kavanagh do all the computer filing. All right—and thanks.'

'Done! Shake on it, Rose.' He smiled, and the familiar impish twinkle danced in his eyes. 'And now for a complete change of subject! What you need is a nice little treat, and it so happens that a grateful gynae patient's husband has given me a timely token of his appreciation. Guess what it is!'

'I haven't a clue,' she said, quite mystified.

'Come closer, and I'll whisper it to you,' he invited,

and as their heads leaned forward over the table, she heard the words, 'Two tickets for the bingo night at St Antony's church hall!'

'Oh, Dr McDowie, I'm afraid such highbrow entertainment is rather out of my league!' she protested in mock dismay.

'Yes, it *is* a bit above your head, I agree, Dr Gillis. What about something a little less ambitious—like two seats for *The Tempest* at the Royal Exchange?'

Rose's eyes widened. She had read the reviews of this prestigious production, and longed to see it.

'Are you serious this time?' she asked.

'Deader than dead serious.'

'Doesn't Tanya want to go?'

'She's on duty tonight, and I'm not quite sure that it's her scene,'

'Tonight? Oh, I can't, I'm on call!' Rose did not know whether to feel sorry or relieved.

'You're not, you know. David Rowan's standing in until we get back. He's as concerned as we all are about you, Rose, and he'll feel damned insulted if you turn down his offer.'

Rose hesitated, smiled, shrugged, and finally shook her head. 'I—I'm sorry, Leigh, but no.'

He leaned forward and spoke very firmly. 'I'm sorry, Rose, but yes. If you don't agree here and now, I'll go and tell your mother. She'll be really upset—she's worried about you being overworked. You're coming to the Royal Exchange tonight.'

She saw that he meant it. 'Well, if you're sure—it doesn't look as if I've got much choice, does it?' she capitulated.

\*    \*    \*

It was a clear, warm evening after another hot day, and a slight breeze stirred the dusty air of the city. The theatre, a brilliantly conceived system of steeply tiered galleries around a circular stage constructed within the old Manchester Cotton Exchange, was a place of magic. Night after night it drew packed audiences to a stylish and sensitive performance of Shakespeare's last play, a complex study of revenge, forgiveness and the approach of old age.

'I always feel that it's like being perched up on scaffolding when I come here,' Leigh remarked, settling himself beside Rose in the back row of the first gallery above floor level. They gazed down on the set of Prospero's island.

'How on earth will they manage to do the shipwreck in the first scene?' wondered Rose, as excited as a child at her first pantomime.

Her question was answered when the majestic sorcerer Prospero held his magic wand aloft, and thunder and lightning exploded all around them. The sound of howling rain and lashing winds filled the air, against a confusion of men's voices and cries of fear. An energetic young boatswain with strangely familiar features shinned up a ladder to the first gallery level and shouted to his crew of dripping wet mariners who appeared from nowhere out of the darkness, holding on to ropes and rigging. A sound of cracking wood was followed by despairing wails, and *The Tempest* had begun.

Rose was caught up into another world where all disbelief was suspended; for the next two enchanted hours her imagination was entirely enthralled by the sorcerer, the young lovers and Ariel the sprite, who flew effortlessly from one gallery to another, singing in a high, piercing counter-tenor of yellow sands and coral reefs.

'I feel as if I'm a completely different person tonight, Leigh,' she whispered.

'Me too. Perhaps we've undergone "*a sea-change, into something rich and strange*",' he quoted softly, his head close to hers and his warm breath on her cheek. She found that they were holding hands at Ariel's command, and was breathlessly aware of his nearness, the clean tang of his aftershave and freshly laundered linen, the touch of his fingers intertwined with hers — and incredibly, the softest of kisses on her cheek when Miranda and Ferdinand declared their love. It seemed as if the Royal Exchange had floated away up into the summer sky, and Rose and Leigh were alone together in a little bubble of shadowy intimacy, enveloped in a timeless spell that had no past, no future, but only a dreamy present, in thrall to Prospero, the very voice of Shakespeare himself, whose presence brooded over all. . .

And Rose was encircled in his arms, his lips found hers, and she responded to a kiss that was sweeter even than Ariel's songs. She drew a long, long breath and surrendered to the sheer sensual enjoyment of it.

When the play was over, and the sound of the prolonged applause at last died away, Rose discovered that there were tears on her cheeks.

'All right, Rosie?' He sounded like Dr McDowie again.

'I don't want to come back to reality, Leigh,' she confided sadly.

He squeezed her arm. 'It was fantastic, wasn't it? In every sense of the word! Come on, Rose, I've got one more surprise for you tonight. Hey, Boatswain! Say, how came you hither?'

And to Rose's amazement the oilskin-clad Boatswain who had appeared in the first and last scenes of the play leapt up the iron staircase to clasp Leigh's hand.

'Hello, old chap! Did you enjoy the — oh, my! What raven-haired beauty have we here, forsooth?'

'Rose, I want you to meet my little brother Andrew,' grinned Leigh. 'Bit-part actor and full-time clown, making his debut at the Royal Exchange!'

'Am I still dreaming?' gasped Rose. 'You didn't tell me that the Boatswain was your *brother*!'

Andrew bent close to her ear. 'Don't tell the doctor, but I was one of the strange shapes as well!'

'I thought you were a fairy,' said Leigh.

'No comment, brother, dear.'

Rose was lavish in her praises of the performance.

'Wasn't Ariel brilliant?' she exclaimed. 'The way he swung from side to side above our heads!'

'Showing us his bare backside,' added Leigh.

'It *wasn't* bare!' she protested. 'He was dressed in flimsy rags and tatters, all greeny-bluey-yellowy.'

'Maybe, but there wasn't much doubt about his gender when he swung a bit close to the front row,' grinned Leigh. 'Reminded me of an undiagnosed breech I caught when I was a student doing my obs at Edinburgh.'

'Our dear parents still can't understand why you chucked a promising career as a physician to go into general practice, you know,' said his brother with a wink at Rose. 'But having seen this sample of the scenery in the baby department, I begin to understand, — mm, yes, mmm —' He ducked as Leigh made a grab at his sou'wester headgear and turned it back to front.

'Just came to the conclusion that I'd rather be a family doctor living alongside my patients—a good mix of ages and backgrounds to tackle on their home ground, rather than spend my life tucked away in hospital,' said Leigh simply. He sighed and glanced at his watch. 'Alas, little brother, we must be on our way back to the other kind of theatre, or we'll turn into pumpkins. I'll catch up with you again at pantomime time. What will you be, Dick Whittington's cat?'

'Yeah, the front legs this year. But I hope to meet Rose again before Christmas.'

'I'll see what I can do. Keep up the good work, and fare thee well!' said Leigh.

'Goodnight, sweet prince—and princess,' said Andrew, planting a kiss on Rose's cheek.

They were silent when they got into the car to drive back to Beltonshaw. Rose's thoughts were distinctly confused as she remembered their incredible shared moment in the theatre. Shouldn't she have heard warning bells ringing somewhere? She made a conscious effort to remind herself of Paul, who had been missing from her mind all the evening.

'Paul will be surprised to hear where I've been tonight,' she remarked.

'You can tell him that Dame Edna Everage is coming to the Palace soon—might be more up his street,' replied Leigh coldly.

'I beg your pardon? As a matter of fact, I quite enjoy the Dame myself, it depends on what mood one is in,' she answered.

'Quite. And the Dame would have to be *very* good to drag Sykes away from Female Surgical right now.'

Rose sat up beside him, tense and frowning.

'What do you mean by that, Leigh? Why are you spoiling a lovely evening?' she demanded.

'Oh, Rose, Rose, how can you let yourself be so used? And insulted by his pandering to that actress and her all-important leg—I bet he's holding it right now!' Leigh could not hold back the bitter words, and Rose was stunned into a shocked silence that remained unbroken for the rest of the drive.

Why should Leigh McDowie suddenly turn so unkind?

A ridiculous idea came into her head. It was surely impossible that he could be jealous? Yet what other explanation could there be for his behaviour?

Dr Rose Gillis was becoming more and more uncertain of her own feelings as she looked back on the magic of *The Tempest*.

## CHAPTER SEVEN

THE preparations for Caroline Trench's farewell party on the last Friday of August were well in hand. An outside catering firm had been booked, and as the long hot spell continued without a sign of a break in the weather, Caroline decided to turn the party into an outdoor barbecue on the green open space at the back of the hospital building.

The guest list grew as celebrities from the television studios were persuaded to put in an appearance, and there was a general mounting of excitement and anticipation as the day approached and at last arrived. The air was hot but sultry, with an ominously breathless stillness. In the morning of that memorable Friday two vans arrived with half a dozen large circular barbecue grills and several hundredweight of charcoal. Trestle-tables were set out in rows on the grass, stacks of plastic chairs were brought out, and an improvised stage was erected with a sound system and microphones, surrounded by a string of fairy lights for after dark.

The party began to be seen as the social highlight of the hospital's year, and publicity for it was encouraged by the management; reporters and photographers from the *Beltonshaw Messenger* were jostled by their rivals from the other local paper, and the name of Caroline Trench attracted freelance photographers who had an eye to the national dailies, including of course the ever-present Roger Maynard.

Rose could not help hoping secretly that her work would prevent her from putting in more than a token appearance at the barbecue, but after the recent hectic spell on Maternity there followed one of those inexplicable lulls with a fall in admissions, and only one delivery took place during the day of the party. She would have offered to change places with Leigh who was on call that night, but yet she felt she should be at Paul's side while Caroline greeted her guests and introduced them to the hospital hierarchy. Mr Mason the consultant surgeon was back from his holiday, so Paul was now more free to enjoy his social life, and Rose knew she should make an effort to fulfil her position as Paul Sykes's — *what*?

Looking at herself in the mirror as she dressed for the occasion, she suddenly asked herself that question: what exactly was she to Paul? Fiancée? Girlfriend? There was a much older word that could be used: *mistress*. Rose frowned. They were unofficially engaged, everybody knew that, and everybody also knew about the caravan at Nethersedge, though it was two months since they had last spent a weekend there. Was it any wonder that Paul had seemed cool towards her lately, and not very free with lifts in his car or visits to her mother? She asked herself if she was being fair to him, but could not come to a decision; a very unwelcome suspicion entered her mind that Paul's interest in her might be dependent on her physical availability, and that without it he had become frankly bored with her preoccupation with her mother and her commitment to the research project. At once she thought of Leigh McDowie and his absorbing interest in both of these concerns; it was becoming increasingly difficult to reckon without this man. . .

She decided then and there to have a straight talk with Paul at the earliest opportunity, to find out exactly what his feelings were. If he still insisted that he loved her, she would ask that their engagement be officially announced, with at least a provisional date set for the wedding.

She looked again in the mirror with a certain satisfaction; in a daringly sleeveless, backless long dress in crimson brocade, she looked simply stunning. Her black hair hung from a centre parting, gleaming and straight except for an upward flick at the ends. Two long crystal earrings flashed fiery rainbows as she moved her head, and her deep blue eyes, fringed by long lashes, held a question in their soft depths. Paul Sykes was not the only man to stop in his tracks as she entered the residency bar for pre-party drinks; Philip Cranstone also registered the impact made by the stubborn young woman doctor, and his wife Annette exclaimed in admiration.

'Oh, darling, is *that* Caroline Trench? Isn't she gorgeous!'

Leigh McDowie came in with Tanya Dickenson on his arm, and for an instant he froze on the spot as their eyes met; Rose caught her breath and remembered the enchantment of *The Tempest*. She beckoned to Paul, and smiled up at him in her most winsome way, needing his confirmation that they were a couple. As they were standing near to Leigh and Tanya, he asked if he could get them a drink. Tanya accepted before Leigh could move away, and they sat down together, a distinctly uneasy foursome. The two men exchanged superficial comments on hospital politics, criticised the administration and discussed the repercussions of the M63 accident seven weeks previously. Rose and Tanya had

little to say to each other, and neither felt inclined to
make much effort, having exchanged the usual compliments about what they were wearing. Tanya wore
lavender-blue culottes that swirled around her slender
ankles, and she looked complacently at ease beside
Leigh, who at one point placed his hand lightly on her
knee as he talked. Rose felt relieved when they got up
to join the guests who were thronging towards the
lighted party area, drawn by the sound of music and
a delicious aroma of sizzling kebabs, sausages and
burgers which rose on the air.

The sun was rapidly sinking and an unexpectedly
chilly breeze had got up; shawls and wraps were pulled
over bare shoulders, and the men needed their jackets.
For so long now the darkening evenings had been very
warm, a series of fine nights under clear, starlit skies;
but now a bank of threatening low clouds was hurrying
across from the Atlantic, and fast approaching the
north-west. The temperature at last began to fall.

The stage was brilliantly illuminated, and Paul was
called to take his place on it with the surgical team and
the nursing staff, together with a few ex-patients who
had received invitations. An enormous cheer greeted
Caroline Trench when she was carried up on to the
stage by Dr Sykes and set down on the chair ready for
her. She looked dazzling in a long white silk dress with
a gold belt, shoes and jewellery. Her abundant red hair
surrounded her head in carefully arranged tumbling
waves; she looked every inch the professional actress.

She shook hands with Mr Mason, and after a few
words of welcome to her guests from the TV series that
had made her a household name, she beckoned Paul
forward.

'Listen, everyone, I want you all to know that Dr

Paul Sykes saved my leg and therefore my career and therefore my life!' she announced, the microphone picking up her words and relaying them to the crowd and far beyond. 'Words cannot express —' Her voice trembled with emotion, and she hesitated before beginning again. 'Words cannot express my gratitude and the special place that Beltonshaw General Hospital will always have in my heart. But above all, my lifelong obligation to this fantastic surgeon who will forever be my friend — ladies and gentlemen, Dr Paul Sykes, my doctor! My wonderful doctor!'

She threw her arms around Paul's neck and they kissed while cameras clicked amidst cheers, whistles and roars of approval from the milling crowd of partygoers.

'Stirring stuff!' remarked Leigh, so close to Rose's ear that she jumped, though he obviously had not seen her.

'All rather sickening, I'd say, and not very nice for Dr Gillis,' said Tanya, causing Rose to stiffen and hold her breath, praying that they would not notice her as Tanya went on, 'You'd think that at least she'd be invited up on to the platform as his — er —'

'I shouldn't worry. A woman as lovely as Rose isn't going to be left on her own for long,' said Leigh in an odd, dry voice that Rose did not know how to interpret. 'Could be that Sykes is in for a shock — anyway, I'm starving. How soon are we allowed to get at the nosh? I could be called away at any time!'

Rose breathed freely again as a surge in the crowd swept them away out of earshot. She resented their comments, yet realised that Tanya had only voiced what she herself felt, and a wave of humiliation brought an angry flush to her cheeks. She suddenly longed to reject Caroline Trench's ostentatious party and return home to her mother and aunt; but Leigh's prediction that she would not be left on her own for long was soon fulfilled.

'*Rose*! How wonderful to see you again! Don't you look super—oh, Rose, how are you?'

And all at once she was surrounded by a group of delighted friends she had not seen for some time. Dr Okoje the anaesthetist and his handsome Trinidadian wife Susannah were accompanied by Dr Lewis Grant, a former anaesthetist now in general practice, and his pretty wife Fay, formerly a midwife at Bolton General and a friend of Rose, who had been her bridesmaid only a few months earlier. Hugs and embraces were exchanged as they were united, and Fay Grant was full of questions.

'Is it really true that you've got Leigh McDowie as your junior SHO on Obs and Gynae? *He* must be stimulating to work with! Has he still got loads of swooning girlfriends? It's a good job you've got Paul Sykes to keep an eye on you, or you could be next in line!' she teased.

'No way!' retorted Rose, though she felt oddly embarrassed by her friend's banter. 'He's seeing a midwifery sister, actually, the one who took over your job on Antenatal—a very cool young woman who knows what she wants and decided on Leigh McDowie as soon as she set eyes on him.'

'Oho! Do I detect a little tiny hint of rivalry?' twinkled Fay. 'A little bird has whispered in *my* ear that the delectable Leigh has been seen visiting the home of his senior SHO, a bossy woman doctor by the name of—er—now, let me see——'

Rose cut in quickly, 'Yes, he *does* visit my home,

Fay, but not to see me. He and my mother have become quite friendly, I mean really close, since she had an operation some weeks ago.'

'Ah, yes, that's right, I'd heard she'd been in Gynae,' began Fay, then stopped in dismay as she saw Rose's expression. 'Oh, my dear, it's nothing serious, is it?'

'Not very hopeful, I'm afraid, Fay.'

'Oh, Rose, I'm so *sorry*! What an awful time for you,' sympathised Fay, her manner completely changed. 'Look, couldn't you bring your mum on a visit to us one weekend? Barfylde's the most heavenly village, and we've decorated the cottage—let me give you a complete rest, Rose!'

'I don't think Mother would really care to leave home, Fay, thank you very much all the same. My aunt—her sister Maura—has come to look after her.'

'Then couldn't you and Paul come for a weekend, just to give you a complete break?' persisted the bright-eyed girl.

'I'd love to, Fay, but right now I feel I can't leave Beltonshaw,' answered Rose, squeezing her friend's arm gratefully. She felt warmed and comforted by the sincerity of real friendship, and walked happily with the Grants and the Okojes towards the tables, where guests were beginning to sit down. Waiters were bringing trays of freshly grilled meat from the barbecues, and the smell was most appetising, though the air was growing chillier and the tablecloths stirred in the breeze. Freak currents of air flicked paper table napkins into the air, spiralling upwards like miniature tornadoes, and the strings of fairy lights swayed to and fro. Across the grass towards them came Caroline Trench, seated in a wheelchair pushed by Paul Sykes and accompanied by a laughing crowd of friends from Granada Television.

'Rose, darling, where *did* you get to? Why didn't you join us on the stage?' asked Paul as he helped Caroline into a chair at the top table and seated himself on her right. He patted the chair next to him. 'You sit here, Rose, with your friends along that side,' he said with an expansive gesture. 'Hi, Lewis, how's life as a GP? Have you met Caroline yet?'

Further down the table on the opposite side Rose could see Leigh and Tanya laughing and joking with Laurie Moffatt and Roger Maynard, who had reaped a rich harvest of photographs to sell to national dailies at a good price. Everybody praised the tasty barbecued fare, though the wind was becoming stronger and ominous trails of ragged cloud streaked across the darkening sky. Paul tucked Caroline's white wrap around her, and Rose was glad she had brought the black-fringed wool shawl that Aunt Maura had crocheted for her as a birthday present.

And suddenly without any warning came a lurid flash of lightning, a jagged fork across the sky that illumined the scene in an eerie blue-white glare for a moment. A gasp went up from the company, and almost immediately a second brilliant flash rent the blackness of the now heavy clouds, followed by the sharp 'crack! crack!' of thunder of a storm centred directly overhead. There had been no preliminary rumbles of its approach, and the whole of Beltonshaw was taken by surprise. Flashes and tremendous claps of thunder continued in the dry air, and Caroline screamed as all the electric lights went out. The deserted stage shook violently in the furious gusts of wind that now ripped at the tablecloths; the scene was changed to one of chaos.

'Go to the boardroom! Go through Maternity!' Leigh McDowie ordered the party guests, standing up and raising his voice as loudly as he could above the din. Paul hastily wheeled Caroline away in her chair, while Rose pointed the way to the Maternity wing, situated at the rear of the hospital building, and therefore their nearest entrance.

As they surged towards shelter, the rain began to fall in huge drops, a deluge sweeping almost horizontally on the howling wind. The rain that had not fallen for almost three months now pounded the parched earth and hissed as it hit the barbecue grills, sending up clouds of steam from the red-hot coals. Windows shook as the rain battered the western aspect of the building, and the partygoers broke into a run, lowering their heads against the driving torrents.

After directing them through the ground-floor corridor of Maternity to the main hospital and the boardroom, Rose dashed into Postnatal, where wildly blowing curtains had swept flowers, newspapers and plastic cups from lockers before the staff could close the windows. Most of the mothers were cradling their babies in their arms while listening to Sister Hicks's description of the air-raids she remembered as a child; she reminded them that there had been *real* danger then, in contrast to a mere thunderstorm, but one or two of them were cowering under the bedclothes in primitive dread of the raging elements.

In the boardroom, Rose found the nursing members of the party busily brewing tea.

'Can somebody go down to the canteen and get some more cups?' asked Sister Banks of Female Surgical. 'We could do with some more milk too!'

Rose obediently set off along the main corridor with

a trolley. Turning into the canteen, she passed the little tea-bar where staff could sit and relax after meal breaks, and wondered if she would find some plastic cups in there.

Opening the door, she came straight upon Paul Sykes and Caroline Trench locked in a close embrace, literally wrapped around each other. She almost ran into them as Caroline gave a little cry and clung tightly to Paul, who raised his head to look at the intruder.

For a moment Rose stood and returned his stare. Then she found her voice, and heard herself actually apologising.

'Oh, sorry! Excuse me — I didn't know there was anybody in here.'

She turned to leave, and caught her ankle sharply on the foot-rest of Caroline's abandoned wheelchair.

'*Damn*!' she muttered involuntarily, and went out, closing the door firmly behind her. She continued on her way to the canteen and proceeded with her errand, returning to the boardroom with the cups and milk.

Later, Rose was to ask herself how she had stayed so calm, and decided that it was because she had not been really surprised. How long had she subconsciously known about Paul's infatuation for Caroline? Perhaps right from their very first meeting on the day of the M63 accident, which had also been the day when she had faced the fact of her mother's illness. For a time she felt no emotion at all, not even hurt or anger; her mind was quite blank as she stood drinking tea and chatting with Fay and Lewis Grant.

It was only much later, when the storm had abated and the guests had departed, that Rose stood at the window of her room in the residency, still in her crimson evening dress, and began to suffer the regret that many a woman experienced when she had to acknowledge that she had given herself too readily to a man who had betrayed that loving trust; she burned inwardly when she recalled the weekends spent at Nethersedge, and it was herself she blamed, rather than the man who had said he loved her.

And what would Leigh McDowie say? Rose put a hand to her face, and wept bitterly.

It was eleven-thirty when Rose eventually wrapped the crocheted wool shawl closely around her and went down the stairs of the residency to ring for a taxi to take her home. The last straggling guests had taken their leave, or had at least disappeared from view, to the medical quarters or the nurses' home. Rose did not wish to meet any of her colleagues, especially Paul Sykes, nor did she feel able to face questions about the party from her mother and aunt. She had waited until she was sure they would be in bed, and intended to creep in quietly without disturbing them.

She lifted the receiver of one of the pay-phones on the ground floor, and with a ten-pence piece ready to hand, she dialled the number. A woman's voice answered.

'Beltonshaw Top Taxi Service — can I help you?'

And then Rose had one of those strange and inexplicable experiences that came to many members of the medical and nursing professions at some time in the course of their careers: a flash of foreknowledge, a premonitory warning that had to be obeyed. Quite suddenly she knew she must not leave the building.

'Beltonshaw Top Taxi Service — can I help you?' repeated the woman's voice with mechanical efficiency.

Rose was tired, depressed and longing for her bed at

home. She needed a taxi to take her there, and yet it was as if an invisible hand covered her mouth, and she did not reply but replaced the receiver on its hook. Closing her eyes for a moment, she leaned against the wall and tried to analyse the reason for her strange behaviour. What on earth should she do now? If she was not going home, where else should she go?

And from somewhere deep in her subconscious mind came the order to go to Maternity *at once*, not to stop to change, but to lose no time. She found herself beginning to run towards the main hospital corridor, her high heels clicking on its mosaic surface. She dashed up the stairs and sped breathlessly into the antenatal and delivery unit section of the department. She stopped for a moment at the office, where an auxiliary nurse was talking frantically on the telephone. Rose's heart missed a beat when she heard the words.

'But are you *sure* Dr Gillis isn't there? Hasn't she arrived home from the party, Mrs Gillis? Oh, I'm sorry, are you her aunt? It's Maternity here. Have you any idea where she ——?'

Rose put her head round the door and gasped out, 'Tell my aunt I'm *here*, Nurse, or she'll be worried sick!'

'It's all right, Miss—er—she's here now, she must have got the message from somebody!' gabbled the nurse in relief. 'I'm sorry to disturb you, but we need her!'

She replaced the receiver and looked apologetically at Rose in her crimson dress, her black hair in disarray, her eyes wide with alarm.

'Oh, Dr Gillis, thank heaven you've come! The Westbrook girl went into labour during the thunderstorm, and didn't tell anybody she was getting pains.

And the police have been on to say that Mr Rowan's been in a road accident and can't come. Mr Horsfield's on holiday in Portugal, so Dr McDowie and Sister Grierson are on their own!'

Rose continued on her way along the corridor, and straight into Delivery Room One. Lynne Westbrook was lying on the delivery bed in the lithotomy position, her legs supported on high, wide stirrups. Angela Grierson stood beside her, comforting her and encouraging her to push downwards. Leigh McDowie, dressed in a sterile green gown and with gloved hands, sat on a surgeon's stool ready to receive the first twin, whose head could be seen advancing. Two cots were prepared, as well as the specially constructed resuscitation cot with its oxygen supply, overhead heater and side-tray of special equipment ready for use. Staff Midwife Pat Kelsey stood waiting with a mucus extractor ready between her lips, and a sterile towel in her hands to take the baby from Leigh McDowie.

Rose's eyes took in the scene at one glance, registering the fact that there was no intravenous drip up, and no paediatrician present. The other immediate thought that came to her was that Lynne's most recent scan had shown that the placenta of the first twin was lying in the lower segment of the uterus, and could therefore separate and cause bleeding, endangering the second twin. Mr Rowan had therefore decided on an elective Caesarean section during the first week of September. And now this had happened. . .

'Terribly sorry to have to send for you, Rose, but thanks a hell of a lot for coming,' muttered Leigh. 'God knows what happened to Rowan, so I asked for you to be called. I'm not too happy about dealing with prem twins.'

'Is the paediatrician coming?' asked Rose.

'Yes, Dr Vane's on her way, and Dr Cranstone's standing by,' answered Angela Grierson. 'Lynne started getting pains about two hours ago, but didn't think it could be labour. Then at eleven-fifteen her waters broke, and we only brought her out of the antenatal ward ten minutes ago — and found the cervix fully dilated. She's had no pain relief at all.'

'Dr McDowie, you carry on delivering the first twin, but do an episiotomy, and make it generous,' ordered Rose. 'Sister, get a drip run through, and I'll put a cannula in for it now. All right, Lynne, my dear, your babies will be small, but we'll take good care of them. Just you do as Dr Leigh tells you, and everything should be perfectly all right. Can somebody do something about my hair?'

'Oh, my God, it's pushing — it's *coming*!' groaned Lynne, straining hard and gripping Angela's hand in frenzied appeal. The efficient sister now showed herself to be a true midwife, comforting and caring for the emotional needs of the young woman who had no mother, no boyfriend at her side during this important moment of her life. Dr Vane burst in at the door, and Leigh concentrated hard on carefully controlling the emergence of the little head. As soon as the face was visible, Pat Kelsey sucked gently through the mucus extractor, the other end of which she applied to the baby's mouth and nostrils. In a matter of seconds the body was born and handed to Stephanie Vane, who had thrown aside her handbag and slipped a green sterile gown over her dress.

It was a boy, and they all smiled when he gasped, flexed his tiny arms and legs, and uttered a plaintive mewing sound as if protesting against this unceremonious change of environment, from the warm darkness of the womb to the touch of air on his skin, amid a jumble of lights and noises. Pat Kelsey immediately labelled him 'Westbrook Twin I.'

Leigh clamped and cut the dangling umbilical cord, and there was an alarming gush of blood.

'We can't give an oxytocic because of the second twin,' whispered Rose in Leigh's ear. 'We don't want the cervix to close yet!' Aloud she said, 'Sorry, Lynne, I'm just going to feel your tummy to see how your other baby's lying.'

As she placed two firm hands on Lynne's tummy, Leigh called out sharply.

'It's all right, Rose, the baby's coming now — oh, hell, *no*!'

To their surprise and dismay, the bulge that now appeared was not the head of the second twin, but the placenta of the first, which flopped out into the plastic dish that Leigh hastily grabbed from the delivery trolley. Another brisk loss of blood followed it.

'Didn't know it was possible for that thing to come out before the second baby,' hissed Leigh in the low tone used by delivery unit staff who always had to remember that their patient was conscious.

'I've never seen it happen before, but I know it can do when it's lying low down,' whispered Rose, who was now faced with a life-and-death decision. 'The trouble is that we now have no time *at all* to play with. The first placental site will bleed like fury.'

'Caesarean? Could you do one, Rose?' he asked her bluntly as sweat ran down his forehead and into his eyes; he wiped his face on the back of his green sleeve.

'No time,' snapped Rose. 'What do you think of the baby's position, Angela? Transverse, isn't it?'

'Yes, it's lying directly transverse,' answered the midwife grimly, because the baby's chances of survival were dwindling with every second that it remained inside, lying across the mother's abdomen. It was impossible to deliver a live baby in that position; either the head or the breech had to descend.

'Get me a gown and a pair of gloves, size six and a half,' rapped out Rose. 'I'm going to attempt an internal podalic version, which means that I put a hand up through the cervix, grab hold of a leg, pull it down and deliver the baby as a breech.'

'Ever done one before?' Leigh asked with a sympathetic grimace.

'No, they're very seldom done these days,' breathed Rose. 'And we shall need to put Lynne to sleep for this.'

'I'll ring the anaesthetist on call,' said Pat Kelsey, turning to the wall telephone.

'No time,' hissed Rose. 'Go into the theatre and get the Boyle's machine. Sister, take an ampoule of Pentothal out of that cupboard and check it with Leigh — and Leigh, you're going to have to be gas-man.'

Her low, rapid orders were immediately obeyed. Angela unlocked the drugs cupboard and handed Leigh a glass ampoule containing a colourless fluid which he drew up into a ten-millilitre syringe; quickly he injected into a vein on the back of Lynne's hand. Meanwhile Pat had rushed out to the maternity theatre, and returned pulling the heavy Boyle's anaesthetic trolley with its cylinders of gas. Lynne's facial muscles relaxed, her eyelids fluttered and closed, her limbs went limp; Leigh grabbed an airway which he fixed between the unconscious girl's teeth, turned on the flow of nitrous oxide and placed a black face-mask over her nose and mouth, attached to the wide, flexible tube through which the merciful gas streamed. It was a simple, basic anaesthetic, but Leigh hoped Rose would be quick; Lynne's pulse and colour were satisfactory, and he slightly increased the amount of oxygen in the mixture. He was aware of his own heart thumping as he concentrated on his crucial responsibility.

Rose uttered a brief, silent prayer as she liberally coated her gloved hand with antiseptic cream. She was sitting on the vacated surgeon's stool and fixed her eyes on Leigh's face as he stood behind Lynne's head. He returned her gaze, and nodded unspoken encouragement.

'I'm putting my hand up through the cervix now,' she muttered. Obstetric practice relied on the sense of touch, not sight, for recognition of internal conditions. 'I've got hold of a limb — an arm? No, a leg, it's got a heel. I'm going to get hold of it and pull it down now.' Speaking aloud helped Rose to concentrate and make decisions.

'Now, here it comes — and there it is,' she breathed, as her hand appeared externally, holding a tiny ankle between her index and middle finger. Leigh nodded silently, and Dr Vane held her breath.

'Thank God it's small, otherwise I couldn't do this,' Rose continued in a silence broken only by the squeals of the first baby, now lying in the resuscitation cot. 'I'm pulling on the leg — and there I can see the buttocks coming down — and it's a girl. Right, now I think I can hook out the other leg — oh, it's come down on its own — see, Dr Vane?'

The baby's bottom and legs now hung downwards, and Stephanie Vane stepped forward to wrap the body in a warm towel.

'Now I'm going to bring down a loop of cord,' said Rose.

'Is it pulsating?' Leigh hardly dared to ask as he supported the mother's chin with his hand.

'Yes, I think so — yes. Now for the anterior shoulder. I can get a finger in the bend of its elbow — and there's the arm out. Now to rotate the body round *this* way, so that the other shoulder comes uppermost — and there it is, both arms out!'

Everybody in the closely knit team hung on her words as she concentrated on the next most crucial stage of a breech delivery: the birth of the head.

'No need for an episiotomy, we've already got one.' Rose's running commentary was addressed to Leigh as she worked with the skill of a more experienced obstetrician. Leigh's role had changed to that of anaesthetist, while the two practising midwives now willingly switched to being highly skilled maternity nurses, working in complete harmony with the two doctors. There was no jealousy, no time-wasting argument about who did what; the contribution of each member was vital, and this was smooth and friendly team-work of the highest quality. Rose knew she could not have accomplished the procedure without the support of them all.

'Hand me the small Wrigley's forceps, Sister. I don't need them for pulling on the baby's head, Leigh, but to prevent it from popping out too quickly, with a too-quick release of pressure — that's how damage can be done. Do you see, I'm placing them so as to form a little cage around the baby's head to protect it and allow it to emerge slowly——'

And as the head appeared in a controlled, unhurried movement, Dr Vane applied the mucus extractor to the mouth and nose. Another faint squeak was heard, and a great sigh of relief went up from everybody.

Leigh never forgot the look on Rose's face at the triumphant outcome of her desperate gamble. He saw her eyes close briefly, and for some reason he noticed and remembered seeing the long crystal earrings trembling with rainbow glints as she looked up and gave a radiant smile in response to his thumbs-up sign.

And so the Westbrook twins were safely delivered before midnight, the boy weighing five pounds and the girl four pounds five ounces. They lay together in the resuscitation cot before Dr Vane took them down to the special care baby unit to spend the first few days of their lives.

The placenta of the second twin was expelled almost immediately, and the total blood loss, though over a litre, was not life-threatening. An injection could now be given to make the uterus contract and stop the haemorrhage, and Rose also ordered a course of antibiotic injections to prevent infection after such a traumatic procedure.

Leigh gave the new mother an inhalation of pure oxygen, and she began to moan and turn her head from side to side.

'All right, Lynne, don't worry, it's all over now,' he said, his deep voice gentle and reassuring. 'You've got two beautiful babies, a boy and a girl. Two little miracles.'

He removed the airway and laid his hand on the girl's forehead. Catching Rose's eye, he added under his breath, 'No kidding!'

The door opened to admit a white-faced David Rowan.

'My God, Rose, what a night! Congratulations on

one hell of a twin delivery,' he gasped when he took in the situation. 'I'm terribly sorry, but I've had to take Eve into Gynae. She's—she's losing our baby, I'm afraid. The poor girl's broken-hearted. We hadn't told anybody yet.'

He went on to tell them that he had taken his wife home from the party in the car, but had skidded on the wet road and run into a lamppost. No other vehicle had been involved, but the car was badly damaged, and Eve's eight-week pregnancy was ending in the gynae ward. David received their shocked condolences with a sigh, but his grateful admiration of Rose knew no bounds. She smiled sympathetically, and sent him back to Gynae to comfort his wife.

After Rose had repaired the episiotomy, Pat Kelsey and Nancy washed Lynne and wheeled her down to the postnatal ward where she could sleep for a few hours and recover from her ordeal before facing the crucial decisions that would have to be made about her babies. Would they be adopted but never forgotten by her? Or would she keep them and bring them up, a full-time occupation and a lifetime's responsibility? This question occupied Leigh's thoughts as he and Rose sat in the office writing up the case-notes of the delivery. Angela Grierson had gone to attend to a new admission. Nancy came in with a tray of tea which she put down on the desk for them.

'Suppose you hadn't come, Rose, and she'd had to rely on *my* skill and experience as an obstetrician?' he reflected wryly. 'That second one could have been dead or brain-damaged, and both Lynne and I would have had to live with that fact for the rest of our lives.'

'We don't know, Leigh. It's useless to speculate about what might have happened,' said Rose seriously.

'Sister Grierson's very capable, and you and she might have coped together, who can say? It was the smallness of the baby that made the internal version possible, and it would be terribly dangerous to attempt it for a single full-term baby which was lying transversely — Caesarean section should always be done. Let's just be thankful that Lynne was in hospital. Suppose she'd gone into labour at home, or while visiting somewhere? I doubt if the girl twin would have made it. There are still a few fatalities with second twins, and probably always will be — just think of all the tragedies there must have been in the past with them.' She sighed deeply, and Leigh picked up her train of thought.

'Yes, those old country doctors and midwives must have seen a lot of tragedies, Rose. Mothers today are fortunate, in spite of all the criticism of the maternity services.'

'Oh, heavens, yes,' she agreed. 'My mother said there was always a "village idiot" in the country district where she was brought up, and a lot of them would have been breech births in primigravidas — some would have been second twins. It just doesn't bear thinking about.'

'You're not a natural childbirth supporter, then, Rose?' he asked with a touch of teasing in his voice.

'Don't jump to conclusions, Leigh — I'm as much in favour of normal deliveries as any member of the Natural Childbirth Trust!' she retorted. 'But that doesn't mean that I'd ever be prepared to take an unnecessary risk with a baby's life — no way! Mother Nature isn't always as kind as her devotees make her out to be, and we should go down on our knees and give thanks for present-day technology when we have need of it.'

'Amen!' he said promptly, and there was a pause. Rose looked at the clock.

'Good heavens, it's gone one! I must get home,' she said, realising how tired she was, and out of place in her evening dress and high heels.

'Just before you go, Rose—tell me, who managed to locate you? We were telephoning all over the place, and I was afraid you might be with—er——'

Rose's face flamed. 'No, I was alone in my room in the residency, and had just decided to go home.'

'So who found you?' he persisted.

She hesitated before replying. 'Nobody. I had a feeling that I ought to look in, that's all.'

'Checking up on me, were you, Rose?' he challenged with a smile.

'Of course not! If you must know, I had some sort of a premonition, and I just knew I mustn't leave the building. Then—well, I just seemed to be drawn towards Maternity. I didn't know that Lynne Westbrook had gone into labour, or that poor David and Eve were in trouble. All I *did* know was that I was needed up here, and fast.'

The look in his dark eyes was absolutely serious as he nodded his understanding.

'That's interesting, Rose, because I was calling out for you in my head, willing you to come. When you walked in I was very thankful, of course, but I wasn't really surprised, you know. We must be telepathic.'

She returned his searching look, hoping he could not see into her mind, and the tangle of emotions there. 'Extra-sensory perception, maybe,' she said lightly. 'Let's say it was the guardian angel of Lynne and her babies who came for me!'

'No, Rose. It was me sending a thought message to *fetch* the angel.'

She was taken aback by his total sincerity, and lowered her eyes.

'Well, it's been a long day, and I don't feel anything stopping me from ringing for that taxi now,' she said a little breathlessly, picking up the office telephone and dialling the outside number. She was told that a taxi would arrive within ten minutes.

'I'll walk down to the entrance with you, Rose,' he said, taking her arm as they strolled along the corridor to the stairs leading to the ground floor and the entrance hall from which the postnatal ward and special care baby unit were approached. It was now in semi-darkness, and all the doors were shut.

'Unusually quiet tonight,' he smiled.

'Yes, after the lull we've had lately, there are only about ten mums in postnatal,' she said, adding with a grimace, 'Philip Cranstone was prowling about in there last night, and poor Doris Hicks was furious because it was so quiet for once!'

'Mm — I can imagine. Isn't that known as Murphy's Law?'

She giggled, and he tightened his hold on her arm.

'Rose, I meant what I said up there. No angel could have been more welcome than you in that delivery room tonight. And the way you sat down and got that second twin out — well, it certainly beat the other party at this place, Rose!'

He leaned towards her as he spoke, and she remembered how he had listened so intently to every word of her 'commentary' during the suspenseful minutes of the internal podalic version and breech delivery, and how she had been supported and strengthened by his presence. How strong this man was! And could it be possible that the sheer intensity of his need for her assistance had summoned her to his side in that mysterious way? She thought of Paul's betrayal, and the bitterness of regret swept over her again. She lowered her face so that Leigh should not see the tears. . .

And then she felt her drooping head being gently drawn towards him and laid against his shoulder. Her face was pressed to the white coat, and his hand stroked the top of her head, smoothing back the strands of raven's-wing hair, freeing it from the elastic band which Pat Kelsey had used to tie it back. Overcome with weariness, disillusionment and reaction from the drama of the Westbrook delivery, Rose hid her face against the smooth linen. She drew a sharp breath and let it out on a sob, just one little choking sound. His arms encircled her.

'It's all right, Rose, my dear — all right, Rosie, love.'

His whispered words and his enfolding arms gave her a sense of security, an awareness that here was a friend she could always rely on. It was a moment of tranquillity, and she revelled in it after all the demands made on her. All tension fell away as she nestled against him.

A ring at the doorbell by the entrance announced the arrival of the taxi. The driver stood on the other side of the glass door, which could only be unlocked from the inside. Rose drew back sharply, pulling her shawl around her and clutching her handbag.

'I must go, Leigh. Goodnight.'

'Goodnight, Rose. Sleep well, and thanks again,' he said gently, stepping forward to open the door for her.

But Rose needed to thank this man for what he had meant to her during their innocent embrace. As she stood in the open doorway she lifted her face and kissed him on the cheek, a friend's kiss of gratitude, a kiss to which Tanya Dickenson could not possibly object.

And because of the taxi driver watching, Leigh could not return it in the way he longed to do, but had to let her go.

## CHAPTER EIGHT

THE thunderstorm broke the long heatwave, and September came in with clouded skies and chilly winds, as if summer had given way to autumn overnight. The first few leaves began to turn colour, and although Cheshire farmers rejoiced at the ending of the drought, the Beltonshaw town-dwellers sensed the melancholy tang in the air that marked the passing of another summer. Children went back to school after the holidays wearing anoraks and wellies, and Brigid Gillis could no longer spend the afternoons lying on her padded chair in the garden. Her strength was now daily diminishing, and Aunt Maura was helped by a community nurse who called in two or three times a week.

Concern for her mother was uppermost in Rose's mind, and she received Paul's phone-call calmly.

'Rose — is that you, Rose?'

'Oh, hello, Paul. How are you?'

'Terrible. I can't begin to tell you how sorry I am for the way you found out, Rose, and I want to —— '

'Found out what, Paul?' she interrupted. 'That you were in love with Caroline? I think I've known it for some time.'

'What on earth do you mean, Rose? How could you possibly know?'

'Look, Paul, we're going to have to go on meeting in the residency and mess, and there's no need for drama as far as I'm concerned. I just hope things will work out well for you, that's all.'

'Rose, I just can't believe you can be so kind, so — so understanding. You make me feel even worse. I need to explain a few things — I owe it to you. Look, could we have dinner together? *Please*, Rose!'

'This just isn't necessary, Paul!'

However, his insistence resulted in a compromise, and she arranged to meet him for lunch on the following Saturday at the Outsiders, a popular wine bar on Beltonshaw main road, not far from the hospital.

Meanwhile Rose was more concerned over the condition of Lynne Westbrook, who remained very poorly for several days after her traumatic delivery, and in spite of antibiotics developed a high temperature and urinary infection. Two pints of blood were transfused on her third day as her blood count was markedly low, but she continued to look pale and listless, with no interest in the life of the ward around her. Only when her distracted parents arrived from Dorset and stood at her bedside did the young woman collapse in tears; newly graduated with a science degree, she was now the mother of two helpless children whose father did not even know they had been born, and could not be contacted on his round-the-world backpacking hike.

Sister Dorothy Beddows was her usual kind and helpful self, and advised Lynne and her parents not to make any decisions until they were calmer and could think clearly. Mrs McClennan, the social worker, saw them in her office, and as soon as Rose heard of the Westbrooks' arrival she hurried to Postnatal and offered to escort them to the special care baby unit, where the twins were thriving on formula feeds.

It proved to be an emotional moment, because both grandparents exclaimed simultaneously,

'He's just like *you*, Graham!'

'She's just like *you*, Hannah!'

And at once the future of the baby brother and sister was decided. Lynne might or might not pursue her academic career, but her mother and father would take care of her children for as long as was necessary; perhaps until she could provide a home of her own for them. Rose was deeply touched by their immediate decision, and she knew that Westbrook Twin One and Westbrook Twin Two would always hold a special place in her own heart.

Paul called at Rose's home to take her out to lunch. She was off duty and he was on an extended lunch-break, a colleague having taken over his bleep for two hours. Rose introduced him to her aunt, and they went into the front parlour, where Brigid lay on the sofa, supported by pillows and cosily wrapped in a hand-crocheted blanket. Paul was shocked by her faded appearance, and a pang of remorse went through him at the thoroughly bad timing of his change of attachment. He chatted as pleasantly as he could with the two ladies, though Brigid had little to say.

Rose was wearing a neat dark wool jersey dress, with a pearl necklace and matching ear-studs. She looked every inch the professional woman, in control of her life and career, independent of any man's protection. In a sense, Paul felt he had never admired her more.

The relationship between them over lunch at the Outsiders was cordial and increasingly relaxed; in fact Rose smiled to herself at the way Paul continued to rave about Caroline, like an eighteen-year-old boy in love for the first time. She listened patiently and with a touch of concern for his future. Caroline was ambitious, and her career was paramount. Whereas Paul and Rose had decided not to marry until he had

gained his Fellowship, it appeared that marriage to
Caroline would be dependent on a film contract and
work on location in Scotland as soon as she was fit
enough. He seemed to be prepared to defer to her
needs and wishes, and she looked to him for everything
concerned with her health and the all-important recovery of her injured leg to full use and movement.

'She's having daily physiotherapy at present,' he told
Rose, who put her fork into another garlic mushroom
and began to feel ever so slightly bored with the subject
of Caroline's leg.

'Tell me, Paul, if I may ask a rather personal
question,' she said with an amused expression.
'Caroline's such a red-haired beauty, and looks
about — er — my age, but just how old *is* she, if I'm
allowed to know?'

'Well, if you promise to keep it to yourself, Rose,
she's in fact just ten years older than you. Yes, I know
it's absolutely incredible, and I don't wonder you're
surprised! It's her marvellous vitality and interest in
everybody she meets that keeps her so young!'

Rose let him drool on, as she had already placed the
actress in the late thirties, and she felt an almost
motherly anxiety for this besotted man who had been
her first and only lover. He was at least five years
younger than Caroline, and his chances of fatherhood
were receding if his new love was in no hurry to get
married.

'So have you a wedding date yet?' she enquired.

'It can't be just yet, Rose, but between you and me
I plan to make her Mrs Sykes by this time next year,'
he confided happily. 'Of course, she'll still be known as
Caroline Trench, and I know our marriage won't

exactly be the conventional "house-and-two-point-four-kids" type——'

You bet it won't! Rose silently agreed.

'—but that sort of life never attracted me anyway. I shall pursue my own career, of course——'

In the shadow of hers, thought Rose.

'—and I've put the caravan up for sale. I can't quite see Caroline roughing it at Nethersedge in her present state, can you?'

'I certainly can't—nor in any other state!' Rose suddenly burst into a peal of laughter that caused other patrons of the Outsiders to turn round and look at them. Paul stared in astonishment for a moment, then he joined in and they shared the joke together. Rose placed a hand over his on the table.

'Oh, my God, Paul, you're so funny!'

'And you're so incredibly sweet and understanding, Rose!'

They went on chuckling, but Rose's smile suddenly froze when she looked past his shoulder and saw Leigh, who had come in with Dr Okoje and his wife Susannah. The expression on his face as he caught sight of them laughing together showed both disappointment and disgust. She saw him mutter to his companions, and they moved over to a corner table on the other side of the bar where they could not be seen. Rose almost felt tempted to go over to him and try to explain the circumstances of the lunch date, but dignity restrained her. What business was it of Leigh's, after all? But her appetite was ruined.

By mid-September the chilly weather had cleared, giving way to a spell of golden autumn sunshine. Mr Horsfield returned from the Algarve, bronzed and refreshed, ready to greet his team with enthusiasm. He promptly summoned Rose to his office.

'You're looking peaky, my dear, and I'm not surprised after what I've heard. You've encountered a few problems while I've been away, and I must congratulate you on the handling of the twin delivery. That little girl will never know how much she owes to you. McDowie has left me in no doubt that you dealt courageously with a very tricky dilemma. Well done, Rose, my dear, well done!'

She flushed with pleasure at the compliment, then replied to his enquiries about her mother. He said he would arrange to call on Mrs Gillis at home to assess her condition.

'And now we come to all your hard work on the survey of postnatal management,' he continued. 'My secretary has shown me a very impressive dossier of information, and I've asked her to convene an early meeting of the obstetric and paediatric teams, so that we can discuss your findings. What about next Wednesday afternoon? I've told Miss Kavanagh to notify every member of the medical staff concerned, and also representatives of the midwives on day and night duty. And I told her to contact a couple of reasonably articulate ex-patients — that Mrs Gainsford if she'll come, and at least one other.'

'I'd appreciate that, sir,' said Rose, a little alarmed at the short notice but delighted by his obvious approval of her efforts.

The two teams gathered for the meeting in the lecture-room of the midwifery training school. Mr Horsfield took the chair, with Miss Kavanagh at his side. Leigh and Rose took their seats opposite Philip Cranstone and Stephanie Vane. Sister Beddows and

Sister Hicks sat with Mrs Gainsford and Mrs Edna Lambert. A buzz of conversation preceded the commencement of the meeting, but Rose's heart fluttered nervously, and she found it hard to reply to Leigh's light-hearted remarks, while Dr Cranstone sat staring across at them with a stony expression. He had surmised that Leigh had modified his views, and might now be as formidable an opponent as he had been an ally. It was a relief when Mr Horsfield stood up to welcome them and proceed with the business of the meeting. To Rose's surprise, he called on Leigh to speak first.

'Let's start with you, Dr McDowie, as I understand you've assisted with Dr Gillis's survey. Are you still as much in favour of supporting Dr Cranstone's policy on postnatal management?'

All eyes turned to the registrar-turned-houseman, who answered with firmness and clarity.

'No, sir. I've undergone a complete change of heart as a result of the survey, and I feel it's most important that the paediatric team should hear and read the information that Dr Gillis has compiled. It's overwhelmingly convinced me that she is right and that Dr Cranstone is wrong, and I'm happy to acknowledge this publicly.'

Philip Cranstone's handsome features hardened into a wary defensiveness, while significant glances were exchanged between the midwives and a seraphic smile spread over Dorothy Beddows's broad, motherly face.

'So! This is a turn-around indeed, Dr McDowie!' said Mr Horsfield, his sharp eyes glinting with amusement behind his gold-rimmed spectacles. 'And is this all the result of reading Dr Gillis's report?'

'No, sir. To be truthful, it was my own small contribution to Dr Gillis's research that changed my attitude, far more convincingly than anything I could have read on the subject,' Leigh went on. 'I did a few night visits to the postnatal ward, and I've seldom experienced such a telling demonstration of the difference between theory and practice.'

Tears sprang unbidden to Rose's eyes at hearing such unreserved and open support; she could not help but feel warmed by his commendation of her work, especially after his former opposition.

'Can you give us some examples of this difference, Dr McDowie?' the consultant invited.

'There are too many to mention, sir—the noise, the constant disturbance of crying babies, the exhaustion of the mothers, newly delivered and in pain from Caesarean incisions and episiotomies, unable to sleep for anxiety about their babies—the staff groping around in the dark while changing babies, trying to avoid putting on the bed-lamps and waking the mothers—oh, it was the whole *atmosphere* of tension and unrestfulness. Put it this way—*I* couldn't sleep in that ward, and after a few nights of it I think I'd go barmy. I wonder there aren't more complaints than there are, quite frankly, and that's very hard on the night staff, who do the best they can in extremely trying circumstances.'

'Thank you, Dr McDowie,' said the consultant non-committally. 'Are there any comments on that?'

In the general murmur of agreement that followed, Philip Cranstone raised a lone voice of protest.

'I have to say that when I visited the postnatal ward in the early hours of the morning, Mr Horsfield, I found the place perfectly quiet and peaceful, as the night sister here will testify,' he said with a determinedly good-humoured smile.

Sister Hicks was not prepared to let this pass without comment, and without asking permission to speak, she demanded to know how many night visits the paediatric registrar had made.

'I looked in for at least an hour on one occasion, and my house officers have frequently been called to the delivery unit at night,' he told her somewhat less convincingly. Mr Horsfield raised his eyebrows.

'Yes, Dr Cranstone, but the delivery unit is not the postnatal ward. One visit of an hour's duration, you said. Miss Kavanagh, will you tell us the number of visits made by the obstetric house officers to the postnatal ward between twelve midnight and six a.m., please?'

The secretary consulted her report and answered precisely. 'Eight visits by Dr Gillis, five by Dr McDowie. Total number of hours — let me see —— ' She turned over a page. 'Total fifteen hours, forty-five minutes in the course of the six-week survey.'

'Thank you, Miss Kavanagh. I'll now ask you to give us some more figures from the report, though we can all read a copy of it at our leisure. Please proceed.'

The secretary read out the relevant figures.

'So let's ask Dr Gillis what conclusions she's reached, based on these findings,' said Mr Horsfield. 'Dr Gillis?'

Rose looked very thoughtful as she faced the company. 'Dr McDowie says he's changed round to my way of thinking when I began the survey, sir,' she said with a little bow of acknowledgement in Leigh's direction. 'In fact, I've modified my *own* opinions, following the research we've both done.'

They all looked at her intently, waiting for her to explain.

'These figures show that just over one third of the mothers still want to have their babies beside them all the time, even during the night, and even after their unrestful experience of the postnatal ward at night,' she went on. 'This is a substantial number, and they mustn't be dismissed just because they're a minority. They're mainly breast-feeders, but include some bottle-feeders. Agreed, Sister Hicks?'

'Oh, yes, Dr Gillis,' nodded the sister. 'Even when we used to take out all the babies at night, there were always some mothers who'd come out to the nursery to check on their babies to see if they'd settled. Mind you, the majority were thankful for a good night's sleep!' she added emphatically.

'Thank you, Sister,' smiled Rose. 'It seems that to take all the babies out at night is as misguided as to leave them all in. The overwhelming conclusion I've reached is that there should be sensible *flexibility* in postnatal management, no hard-and-fast rules, and an acceptance that every mother and every baby is a separate individual. We therefore need to re-open the night nursery, currently being used as a store-room, and it should be available for all the mothers, but— and this is a big but—the choice should be the *mother's*, and not that of the obstetricians, nor of the paediatricians, nor of the midwives, though the mid-wives are in the best position to give guidance to a mother who's unsure what to do. They're on the spot, actually *with* the mother round the clock, as opposed to the medical staff. Thank you!'

Rose sat back, flushed but satisfied with her conclusions. Leigh smiled his approval, but Philip

Cranstone looked like a man who had had his guns spiked; he had intended to accuse her of having no point of view but her own, but she now advocated compromise.

'Are there any further comments from our midwives?' asked Mr Horsfield.

'Yes, sir,' said Dorothy Beddows promptly. 'A mother should feel that she's free to *change her mind* on both issues, breast-feeding and rooming-in. With her emotions in turmoil, she may feel quite differently after a few days of rest and readjustment to her new situation.'

'Ah, yes, that's a woman's traditional prerogative, to be able to change her mind,' agreed Mr Horsfield, his eyes twinkling. 'Perhaps we can now ask our two ex-patients to give us the benefit of their experience. Mrs Gainsford?'

Mrs Gainsford reported with satisfaction that after taking her own discharge, she had rested at home while her baby had been bottle-fed by her mother-in-law. However, she was now breast-feeding again, though her community midwife had advised giving a formula feed at the end of the day when her milk supply tended to be lower, and so ensure a reasonably quiet night.

'Once I was away from the stressful atmosphere of that ward, I found that my lactation began to increase, and I'm now a proper mother!' she said proudly.

'With the assistance of that supplementary feed at night,' Rose reminded her. 'Don't forget that Sister Hicks advised this until your own milk was sufficient for the needs of a large baby.'

Then Mrs Lambert was asked to speak.

'After my Caesarean, I felt very much under the weather for two or three days, and certainly not well enough to look after my little girl,' she said. 'I might as well admit that I wasn't eager to breast-feed, and as she was doing well on the bottle, I let her carry on. I don't think I'm any less of a proper mother because of this — in fact I'd like to make a special plea that mothers shouldn't be made to feel guilty just because they don't breast-feed,' she finished on a breathless note, having rehearsed her little speech by heart.

'Thank you both,' said the consultant. 'So where does this leave us? I think Dr Gillis got the right word when she said *flexibility*. As in most areas of life, we need to compromise, to have the grace to admit that there'll always be another point of view, right? What have you got to add, Dr Cranstone, regarding Dr Gillis's report?'

'Obviously I can't produce any new arguments in the face of such an impressive array of figures,' said the paediatrician with a touch of sarcasm. 'We're all aware, I hope, of the enormously superior qualities of breast-milk over formula — the correct balance, the right temperature, immediate availability, the antibodies which give early immunity to infections, the saving of time and money, and of course the special bonding relationship between the mother and child. Having had recent happy experience of all these benefits to my own child, I've come to the conclusion that I'm more fortunate than I supposed. In any case, I have no wish to prolong friction between our teams,' he ended with a half-hearted gesture of co-operation; Philip was used to being popular, and did not relish being thought a bad loser.

'Thank you, Dr Cranstone,' said the consultant. 'Well, I've learned something from Dr Gillis's hard work, and I trust that we all have. I shall see that her report is publicised in the right quarters. Now we must

act on it. In future there's to be freedom and flexibility
in place of a too-rigid policy. The night nursery will be
re-opened by the end of this week. Is that quite clear?'

There were smiles and sighs of relief. Philip
Cranstone looked at his watch, murmured something
about an appointment, and left without further comment. The meeting was declared closed, and Rose found
herself being congratulated on all sides. When Leigh
complimented her again on the honest and unbiased
presentation of her report, she flushed with pleasure,
taking his hand and smiling up into his face with joy.

The spell was broken when Tanya Dickenson swept
into the room.

'Is it over? Can I speak with you, Leigh?' she asked,
her light blue eyes alight with anticipation. She looked
very attractive in a white trouser suit, her silver-blonde
hair tied in a ponytail with a blue ribbon.

'They're holding the auditions for the hospital's
Christmas pantomime!' she announced. 'It's going to
be *Sleeping Beauty* this year, and it's a simply marvellous script by that charge nurse on Intensive Care —
lots of digs about mismanagement of the National
Health Service, and so witty! Only we're waiting for
*you*, Leigh, to audition for the part of Prince
Silversword, the hero who comes and cuts his way
through all the red tape to wake the Princess of Health!'

'But shouldn't a girl play the Prince?' asked Leigh.
'I mean, the principal boy is traditionally a female,
isn't he? — she? — it?'

'No, we want a *proper* Prince, terribly strong and
fearless!' smiled Tanya. 'And one who can sing to his
own accompaniment on the guitar. There's absolutely
nobody else but you to do it. Oh, come on! I've just
auditioned for the part of the Sleeping Beauty, and got

it!' she added with a modest bow that did not disguise her excitement.

'Oh, well, that settles it, I suppose! Let's go and get it over, then,' Leigh agreed, allowing himself to be dragged away by Tanya, while Sisters Beddows and Hicks laughed and applauded.

Rose managed a smile, but felt a chill in her heart which had been so warmed by his support. Tanya was obviously in love, and, as long as she was around, Leigh might as well be ten thousand miles away.

Mr Horsfield was true to his word, and on the day after the meeting, he made a domiciliary visit to Brigid Gillis. After examining her, they discussed the situation over tea and scones provided by Aunt Maura.

'How are you keeping, Miss Carlinnagh?' he asked. 'Are you getting enough rest and eating properly? Is the work not too heavy for you?'

'Sure, I've managed very well so far, Doctor,' answered Maura, 'and for meself I'm fine and willin' to see after poor Brigid—in fact it's me hope that she'll be able to stay here in her home until—until——'

Her voice broke, and Rose got up and put her arms around her aunt, equally unable to speak.

'Try not to distress yourself, my dear,' said Mr Horsfield gently. 'Your sister is evidently receiving first-class care, and my only fear is that you'll tire yourself out. I shall speak to Dr Tait about asking the community nurses to come in daily from now on, but as long as you're willing and able to look after your sister at home, I'm more than happy to agree.'

'Thank ye, Doctor, it's good o' ye,' whispered Maura, wiping her eyes. 'Would ye be wantin' another cup o' tea now?'

Driving back to the hospital, the consultant attempted both to warn and to reassure Rose.

'Just remember, my dear, if you feel your aunt is getting too tired, or if you feel that your mother needs more specialised care, you have only to tell me, and she can have her single room in Gynae. Don't hesitate, Rose — I rely on you to monitor the situation at home.'

Rose could only nod in acknowledgement, and he patted her hand. 'Good girl.'

September gave way to October with its misty mornings and the first frosty nights. Rose's long hours as a junior doctor were made easier for her by Leigh and David Rowan, who took over her duties as much as they could, and it was also a great relief to be finished with the research survey. Rose delighted in the now relaxed atmosphere of the postnatal ward and the re-opened night nursery. The mothers were free to make their own decision whether or not to use it, and the quiet, restful nights meant that they were far more ready to face the daily routine of feeding, changing and bathing their babies. Without their feeling pressured to breast-feed, the number of successful breast-feeders actually went up; Sister Hicks could once again enjoy her work, and smiled approvingly whenever she saw either Dr Gillis or Dr McDowie, though the latter was now busily involved with rehearsals for *Sleeping Beauty*, and had very little free time. He still managed to pay brief visits to Brigid and Maura, and insisted that Rose saw her mother at least once a day, even if it meant taking over her bleep when she left the hospital. She realised that her feelings towards him had undergone a significant change, and when she allowed her thoughts to stray in his direction, she admitted to herself that he had become part of her life, a friend whom she could never forget, no matter what the future might hold. She relied on him; she leaned on his strength. If she ever asked herself secretly what more she felt towards this man, she tried to suppress the answer. Tanya Dickenson had a prior claim on him, and her beauty and talent must surely be more attractive than another man's discarded mistress could ever be. Rose tried to dismiss her treacherous longings and concentrate on devoting herself to her mother and to her work, but there were times when the going was difficult, and the effort to hide her emotions took all her professional cool.

Entering the antenatal ward office one afternoon when the unit was quiet, she found Leigh and Tanya going through their script together.

'Oh, *good*, you can prompt us, Dr Gillis!' cried the lively blonde girl, eyes dancing as she gazed at Leigh with all the pride of possession. 'He's just hopeless at learning his lines, and the dress rehearsal will be here before we've learned our parts! Here's the script, see — start at the bottom of the page — ready, Leigh?'

Rose avoided his face as she picked up the dog-eared, Biro-marked sheets of paper.

'Go on, then, Prince Silversword,' she said brightly, forcing a smile, and Leigh began the speech, his dark eyes dancing with merriment.

'To this entangled spot I'm led,
Wastepaper Castle looms ahead.
Here patients needing treatment wait
'Midst endless forms in triplicate.
My silver sword I now unhook
To cut through all this gobbledegook!'

'Good, now you have the fight with the two evil fiends, Closure and Cutback,' prompted Tanya, 'and at last you arrive in the room where I — where the Sleeping Beauty lies.'

Leigh gave Rose an almost imperceptible glance, but she was concentrating on the script, her raven-black head bowed over the paper on the desk. He went on,

'Thanks to my shining scalpel blade
I've found again my lovely maid.
Bewitched, she lies in coma bound —
The kiss of life will bring her round!'

'Go on then,' giggled Tanya, closing her eyes provocatively. He quickly kissed the tip of her nose, and she pouted.

'*That's* not very romantic, is it, Dr Gillis? Try to put a bit more feeling into your part, darling! Now I wake up and say:

What sudden dream of sweetest bliss?
Methought I felt a prince's kiss.'

Leigh replied rather unsteadily, trying not to laugh,

'It is no dream that wakes thee, dear,
Your lover Silversword is here —
And will with better use of wealth
Restore you to your National Health!'

Tanya blushed and fluttered her long lashes.

'Full gladly will I be thy bride,
And through our kingdom we shall ride.
Then all the patients will rejoice —
Doctors and nurses, raise your voice!'

Leigh gave an unmusical roar of 'Daddy wouldn't buy me a bow-wow!'

'Oh, darling, don't mess about, or we'll never get it right!' Tanya scolded, though she smiled complacently as she turned over the page. 'This is where you pick up your guitar and lead the full company into the final medley, starting with "True Love". How does it sound to you, Dr Gillis?'

'Bloody awful, I should think,' cut in Leigh quickly. 'Look, Tanya, we can't waste Rose's time any longer with this drivel. By the way, do you want to pop home for half an hour, Rose?' he asked seriously.

'Not just now, thanks,' she smiled, determined to be pleasant if not wildly enthusiastic about their efforts. 'You'll be a smashing Sleeping Beauty, Tanya! If you'll both excuse me, I just want to look in on Postnatal and ask about Sister Beddows's daughter — she should be due in any day now.'

And so she got herself away from the Sleeping Beauty and her Prince Silversword, a couple who seemed to be as much in love off stage as on.

Rose felt the lack of a good woman friend in whom she could confide, and she looked forward to a chat with Dorothy Beddows over a cup of tea in the postnatal ward office; however, an excited young staff midwife greeted her with the news that Sister had been called up to the delivery unit where her daughter Philippa had just been admitted in labour with her first child. Glad to have something else to think about, Rose went back upstairs to introduce herself to Philippa and her husband Lance, a good-looking young man. Dorothy hovered anxiously over her daughter, and Sister Pardoe was doing her best to calm the prospective grandmother.

'Come on, Dorothy, I'm taking you over to the staff canteen for tea while Sister prepares Philippa for labour,' Rose insisted, acknowledging the Scottish midwife's grateful look as she dragged Dorothy away.

Philippa was only in very early labour, and, after being snugly installed in Stage One Room B, she was encouraged to walk around the unit with Lance, take a bath, watch television and not to expect any exciting developments for several hours. Rose persuaded Dorothy to spend her evening off at home having a rest before whatever events might take place during the night — and she herself was ordered by Leigh to go and say goodnight to her mother after supper while he took over her bleep.

'But it's your night off!' she objected as she looked up into his dark eyes that were full of — what, exactly? Sympathy? Authority? A little of both, perhaps. Rose could not be sure what his expression held, but she hoped fervently that her own whirling emotions were well hidden under a matter-of-fact exterior.

'Off you go, Rosie, and don't hurry back,' he said lightly. 'Give Brigid a kiss for me — like this — ' And just for a moment there was a butterfly touch of his lips against her forehead.

Rose rang for a taxi and within fifteen minutes was at her mother's bedside. It was eight o'clock, and quite dark, though the sky was clear and there was a full moon. Maura told her with great satisfaction that Father Naylor had visited during the afternoon, and had talked for some time in private with Brigid.

'She made her confession, and then we both had holy communion from that good priest,' Maura whispered. 'It was a great comfort, so it was.'

Rose spent half an hour sitting beside her mother, who seemed extraordinarily calm and contented. Not many words were exchanged between them, but when Rose passed on Leigh's message of love and gave Brigid his gentle kiss on her forehead, the blue eyes softened with a special tenderness.

'Oh, and isn't himself the lovely man, Rose — he'll take care o' ye, daughter — the lovely man. . .'

Rose smiled and took hold of the transparently thin hand.

'I must go now, Mother. Goodnight, darling, and God bless you. Sleep well tonight.'

'Goodnight. . .goodnight, my daughter.'

'I love you — Mummy.'

Rose was always to remember the loving smile that illumined Brigid's face as they made their farewell. Then the taxi was at the door, and she kissed Aunt Maura and returned to the delivery unit and a visit to the gynaecology ward before going to her room in the residency.

Two other babies were born that night before Philippa was eventually delivered. Sister Angela Grierson did not need any doctor's assistance, and supervised both deliveries, the first with a student midwife, the second with one of the new medical students from the University Hospital. As Philippa was the daughter of a staff member, Angela did not delegate her care to a student, but took complete responsibility for the delivery herself.

Rose slept for several hours before being summoned to the delivery unit as she had requested when Philippa was in stage two of labour. A tired Lance and a very anxious Dorothy greeted her as she came in, but she had no intention of taking over Angela's role; indeed, as she watched the sister's neat, methodical movements, she reflected that there was no better way to have a baby than to be in the hands of a capable, caring midwife.

'Come on now, Philippa — give me another strong push, there's a good girl!' encouraged Angela as the panting girl clung to her husband with one hand and her mother with the other. 'And another push — come on, you can do better than that! And again — good, that's better — your baby's nearly here!'

'Give it all you've got, my love, the winning-post is in sight!' pleaded Lance.

'Oh, Philippa, my little girl, don't worry, your mammy's here!' wailed Dorothy, and Rose suppressed a smile of sympathy for Sister Grierson; the most professional doctors and nurses could be amazingly unhelpful when the patient was a close relative.

'Well done, Philippa, do as Sister tells you,' she said discreetly.

And at a quarter to six, just before the very first rays of the autumnal dawn appeared in the eastern sky, a beautiful little girl entered the world, to the joy of her parents and grandmother. Her sloe-black eyes opened wide as Angela wiped the soft fuzz of wet black hair, and handed her to Philippa before cutting the umbilical cord.

'Oh, she's the most beautiful baby in the world!' cried Dorothy ecstatically.

'That's why we're calling her Bella,' grinned Lance, leaning over to kiss his wife and daughter.

Bella's strong, lusty cries filled the delivery room, mingling with the sounds of laughter, tears and words of congratulation. There was also the sound of a distant telephone ringing in the office, but the happy occupants of the room neither heard nor heeded it.

It was only when the auxiliary nurse put her head round the door that a hush fell upon them all, except for Bella, whose piercing cry continued as the nurse gave the message.

'It's for you, Dr Gillis, an urgent call. I'm sorry, but you're to go straight home, love.'

# CHAPTER NINE

THE end had been entirely peaceful, for Brigid had slipped quietly out of the world in her sleep, and had been found by her sister, who had woken suddenly at half-past five, conscious that she was now alone in the house.

As Rose looked down at the calm and tranquil beauty of her mother's face, free at last from pain and anxiety, she breathed a prayer of thankfulness that Maura's wish had been fulfilled, and that Brigid had been able to remain in her own home. Rose opened the top window, and heard a blackbird's song close by in the garden. She stood looking out at the October sky and the fallen leaves, feeling she ought to be able to weep, but she remained dry-eyed and empty inside.

Gradually the sound of a man's deep voice intruded on her ears; he was speaking to Maura in the kitchen. At first she thought it was Dr Tait, their GP, but then to her absolute amazement she recognised the unmistakable tones of Leigh McDowie. Unable to restrain herself, she ran into the kitchen, and was immediately gathered into his arms. For a long moment he held her in silence, and her tears began to flow, reaching a crescendo of agonising sobs. He stroked her dark head as he had done before at moments of emotional intensity, whispering to her with words of comfort.

'There, my love, all right, it's all over now — she's all right, Rosie, love,' he repeated with soothing gentleness.

'Why are you here?' she mumbled incoherently against his jacket.

'I asked to be called whenever this happened, Rose. David Rowan will move into the Residency for a couple of days, and there's a locum SHO coming in for two weeks. Don't worry, the old man and I have got it all in hand,' he reassured her. 'I'm available to you for all of today, at your service with my car. We'll make all the arrangements together.'

Her heart swelled with gratitude for such kindness and practical support from her colleagues, especially this extraordinary man who always seemed to appear out of nowhere whenever she needed a friend at hand. While Maura made tea and toast, Leigh mentioned all the formalities that would have to be attended to: a medical certificate from Dr Tait, contacting the undertaker, and the registration of the death at Beltonshaw Town Hall. Again he promised he would be at her side throughout the day.

'I really feel quite lost about some of the things that have to be done,' Rose confided sadly. 'Especially the business about the Registrar.'

She was looking down as she spoke, so did not see the flicker of deep pity that passed across Leigh's face, a look of real dread in his eyes as he contemplated what she had still got to face, and his own reluctant part in it.

'The trouble is, you see,' she went on, 'that my mother kept all her papers in a strong metal box on top of her wardrobe, and it's always been kept locked. I have no idea where the key is, and heaven only knows how I'm to——'

She stopped speaking and stared at his hand held out

in front of her. In the middle of his palm lay a large black iron key.

'Is that it?' she cried, turning to look full into his face. He nodded, and she remembered the day she had come home unexpectedly, to find him going through private papers with Brigid. Her face flamed. 'Did my mother give it to you?'

He nodded, and there was compassion in his eyes for her. 'Several weeks ago, Rose.'

'But *why*? Why not me, her daughter? Oh, for God's sake, Leigh, why did she never trust *me* with her papers?'

'Sssh, Rose, quiet! Not in front of Maura,' he commanded with total authority. 'Listen, love, after we've seen the GP and the undertaker, I'm going to take you out for a quiet drive. We have to talk.'

'But with all that there is to be done ——' she began, unable to understand his persistence but grateful for his strong presence.

It was gone ten o'clock when they set out for their drive. Leigh told Maura he was taking Rose to attend to some private legal business of her mother's, and, after settling her in the passenger-seat with a rug over her lap, he drove out into the Cheshire countryside, rich in mellow October colours. Through winding lanes and between stubbled fields where flocks of starlings swooped in circles against the clear sky, they arrived at the entrance to Dunham Massey, a fine family mansion acquired by the National Trust, where they could walk in privacy and at leisure beneath the horse-chestnut trees with only a herd of deer for company.

Getting out of the car, he opened the passenger door and offered her his arm.

'We'll walk through the park,' he said.

'What's this all about, Leigh?' she demanded as she got out. 'What do you have to tell me?'

'Something she never wanted you to know, Rose,' he told her, tightening his hold on her arm as he led her over the steps and into the deserted park. The trees were a blaze of red, gold and bronze, and the glossy horse-chestnuts hung in clusters above them.

'Go on,' she said breathlessly. 'Say what you have to say!'

A growing sense of apprehension made her voice shrill. He felt for her gloved hand and entwined his fingers with hers.

'Rose, I know the contents of your mother's strong-box. She did me the honour of showing it to me and sharing a secret with me. It was entirely her choice, Rose. I never influenced her in any way.'

'So tell me, Leigh — *what's* in the damned box, then?'

'Well, there's her birth certificate which you'll need to take to the Registrar,' he began.

'Well, I know *that*, of course,' she said impatiently. 'I shall need the marriage certificate too — and *I* have to be the person to register her death, being her next of kin, so even though you've been entrusted with these documents you'll have to hand them over to me.' There was a trace of bitterness in her voice.

'Rose, my dear, I'm surrendering the key to you *now*,' he said. 'Here it is — take it. Your mother had her reasons for keeping her private papers hidden. You have your own birth certificate, of course ——'

'What on earth has *my* birth certificate got to do with all this?' she asked in mounting agitation.

'You'll have noticed that yours is one of the short-ened forms, and only gives your name, sex, date and place of birth,' he said gently.

'That's right, the shorter certificates had only recently come out when my birth was registered,' she agreed. 'Leigh, what's all this leading up to?'

He drew a deep breath. 'There's no marriage certificate, Rose.'

'*What*? What are you talking about?' she cried, stopping in her tracks and looking up at him.

'Your mother was never married, Rose.'

The words hung in the still air between them.

'Of course my mother was married!' she almost shouted. 'My father was a sailor, Able Seaman James Gillis — how dare you say she wasn't married?'

She stepped back from him, wrenching her hand away from his hold.

'Oh, my God, Rose, this is just the sort of reaction that Brigid so much dreaded,' he sighed. 'This is why she never told you. Poor dear woman.'

She stared at him wildly. 'This can't be true, it can't, it can't! Her name was Mrs Gillis, and my father was James Gillis!'

'For heaven's sake, Rose, just *listen*, will you? Yes, your father *was* James Gillis, but they were never married. Brigid was a good woman, a devoted mother, a courageous lady in every way, except that she couldn't bring herself to tell you the truth — and if *this* is how you behave, I'm not surprised.'

He took hold of her shoulders and spoke quietly, insisting on her attention.

'Your mother changed her name from Carlinnagh to Gillis when she left Ireland and came to Liverpool. There's a certificate of deed poll to prove the legality of the name change, and none of your Carlinnagh relatives know that she was never married, not even Maura. And you're not to tell your aunt, Rose. I

promised Brigid on my word of honour that her family
would never know, but there was no way I could keep
it from *you*.'

Rose looked up at him with eyes that were blurred
with tears. He released his grip on her shoulders and
took her arm again, to continue their walk through
Dunham Park. She did not resist, but held on to him
as if to keep herself from falling.

'Your mother sacrificed her whole life to you, Rose,'
he went on. 'There's nothing for you to be ashamed of
on her behalf. She was a very brave woman, and only
feared one thing—that you'd condemn her if you ever
found out. Doesn't it sound ridiculous in this day and
age, when nearly half our maternity patients are single
girls or co-habitees? But your dear mother grew up
against an Irish rural backwater where unmarried
mothers just weren't accepted. Think of it, Rose—she
was twenty-nine, a quiet, respected schoolteacher, the
eldest daughter of a strict Catholic family. And then
she fell in love.'

Rose covered her face with her free hand.

'Was he *really* a sailor, then?' she asked shakily.

'Yes, an able seaman on leave, and his name was
certainly James Gillis. When he rejoined his ship, she
tried to contact him, but all she got was a letter from
his captain, telling her that he'd been drowned in an
accident at sea. That letter is also in the strongbox.'

'Didn't he have—parents that she could have gone
to see?' Rose asked, tears running down her cheeks.

'No, my dear. He'd come from a Liverpool children's
home, straight into the Navy—there just wasn't anybody. He must have been a lonely young man, a few
years younger than Brigid. It was the most terrible pity
that just as they'd found happiness in each other——'

Leigh sighed deeply, and continued to hold Rose close to him as they walked.

'Anyway, when she realised she was pregnant, she told her family she was going to meet Gillis in Liverpool. In due course she wrote to tell them she was married, and later that she'd got a daughter but that she was widowed. Oh, Rose, what that girl must have gone through during the months before you were born! A most remarkable lady—you should be proud of her. I know I would be.'

Rose shivered and stared down the long tree-lined avenue curving round towards the house. Her voice trembled when she spoke.

'Thank you, Leigh. I'll need time to take all this in, but what you've told me does explain a lot about my relationship with my mother. She never talked about the past, even when I asked her to tell me about my father. And now I know why she kept on saying "Forgive me" when she was recovering from the anaesthetic. Oh, but *why* didn't she tell me before she went?'

'You might as well ask why don't we all tell our parents about our *own* relationships?' Leigh pointed out quietly.

Rose turned her head with a sharp movement.

'I suppose you're talking about Paul,' she said harshly. 'How right you are! Mother never knew!'

Leigh considered his next words very carefully.

'My dear girl, I've had intimate relationships with girlfriends, but I've never told my parents the details,' he said with a wry smile. 'It's a taboo subject between parents and children. Come on, Rose, you've got to be brave now, like your mother. We'll go and see the Registrar together, and only he and you and I will ever know poor Brigid's secret—nobody else in the world!'

Except for Father Naylor, thought Rose, and she felt a sudden glow of comfort at the remembrance of the priest's kindness and her mother's calm farewell the previous evening.

'All right, Leigh, let's go. I'm ready now,' she told him. 'Thank you for telling me. It was a terrible job for you, and I'm sorry you got landed with it.'

His only answer was to encircle her with his arm as they walked back to the car. How glad she was to lean on this man in whom her mother had chosen to confide, knowing he would later have to reveal the truth to the daughter she had been unable to tell. Rose sorrowed in her heart when she contemplated what Brigid's lonely pregnancy must have been like. Had the thought of abortion ever crossed her mind? Rose was quite sure it had not. And adoption? Perhaps — but only to be dismissed when the baby girl lay in her arms, all that she had left of that brief flowering of passion, the only lover she had known.

Rose stole a look at Leigh's profile as they went along, and was thankful that Brigid had found such a trustworthy friend during her final months.

Rose insisted on returning to work the week after the funeral, as there seemed to be no point in staying at home brooding alone when what she really needed was the consolation that came from serving the needs of others.

The funeral had been a turning point in her desolation after the double blow of losing her mother and discovering the truth about the past. Mr Horsfield had attended the ceremony, as had several other members of the medical, midwifery and gynae staff; she had walked between Leigh McDowie and her weeping aunt as they had followed the coffin into St Antony's church. Afterwards the ever-dutiful Maura had served tea, sandwiches and cake to the small party of friends who had returned to the house, which was full of flowers and cards with messages of sympathy. Rose had experienced a merciful lightening of her sadness, and as she looked up into the clear blue sky when the last guests had departed, the conviction came to her that life must go on, and that there was still work to be done and happiness to be found in the company of friends; so as soon as she had accompanied Maura to Liverpool, parted with a loving embrace on the quayside, and watched her sail away into a grey mist over the Irish Sea, Rose donned her white coat and the reassuring smile of a doctor.

It was a relief to be back in harness, and, without the need to leave the hospital each day, she begged Leigh to allow her to take over his bleep for the occasional hour or two, to enable him to attend rehearsals for the pantomime and learn his lines.

'Please, Leigh, I might just as well stay on call this evening, I've nothing else to do, and I feel better when I keep occupied,' she said, smiling—and, somewhat against his better judgement, he often accepted her offers. The truth was that Leigh was beginning to realise that he had a personal dilemma of his own that would not go away; in fact he admitted to himself that something would have to be done about it. There was no doubt that Tanya was more than a little fond of him, and his conscience pricked him because he had let himself be led on by her frank encouragement from his first day as SHO on Obs and Gynae. It had been a kind of defence on his part against the mounting fury and frustration he felt at witnessing Rose's liaison with Paul

Sykes, and knowing of their unofficial engagement. No man with any pride could have hung around in her shadow while Sykes was so openly preferred, but things had changed since then. Sykes was infatuated with the actress, and Leigh's relationship with Rose had developed in a special way, both through working closely together and because of her mother's partiality for him, and all the consequences of that. He now had to face up to his own true yearnings, and ask himself whether any circumstance was important enough to risk losing even a chance of happiness with the only woman he truly loved.

So what prevented him from rushing to her side and telling her so? There were two main reasons why he felt he should wait. Firstly, he was by no means sure that Rose returned his love, and in her present emotional turmoil he was reluctant to confuse her further with a declaration of love, but felt he should wait until she was more settled and sure of herself. Sykes might be distracted by Caroline Trench, but Leigh had no evidence that Rose had ceased to love him—and if Caroline should tire of him, or find somebody more congenial to her tastes, Leigh could imagine a situation where Paul could return thankfully to Rose, who might be overjoyed to take him back.

Secondly, there was Tanya. She was enjoying every moment of their rehearsals together, both in public and in the semi-privacy of the library in the residency. He had resisted her attempts to get invited to his room, and in fact had given her no real cause to suppose that he returned her open adoration. True, there had been a few shared meals, usually in the company of friends like Laurie and Roger, and routine goodnight kisses; but the intimacy of *Sleeping Beauty* was becoming an embarrassment, and he knew that in the end he would have to be cruel to be kind. Colleagues were looking on them as an established couple, an image that Tanya was more than happy to maintain.

I shall have to speak to Tanya and let her down gently if I can, he thought ruefully, but decided to wait until after the pantomime. It was scheduled for two performances in early December, and Leigh hesitated to upset the all-important heroine so close to the opening night. It could even wreck the show. But as soon as the show was over. . .

November brought the surprise announcement of an engagement between Dr Paul Sykes and Caroline Trench. Nobody knew who had leaked the information to the Press, but national newspapers carried photographs taken by Roger Maynard of the actress and her doctor fiancé. The gossip columnists got to work on digging into Caroline's past, and came up with a former marriage to a policeman and a son who had reached the embarrassingly advanced age of nineteen, living with his father and stepmother. Both Caroline's ex-husband and son had little comment to make about her engagement to the young surgeon.

Leigh's reaction was as quick as it was indignant. As soon as he had seen the newspaper in the mess at lunchtime, he approached Rose and started a conversation with her, joking pleasantly about recent activities in the maternity department. When they left to go to the afternoon session in the antenatal clinic, he took her arm and swept her past Paul's table, ignoring the surgeon's tentative, 'Hi, you two!' as he very publicly tore up the newspaper and threw the pieces into the litter-bin by the door as they went out.

Still holding her elbow while they walked towards the outpatients department, he tried to speak comfortingly to her.

'What an idiot poor old Sykes has made of himself, Rose! The guy's obviously gone completely off his nut. I don't want to speak out of turn, but however you may feel about all this now, you're well rid of him, love.'

She was touched and even a little amused by his awkwardly offered sympathy.

'Oh, I've known for weeks that he and Caroline were eventually planning to marry, but I wasn't expecting an announcement so soon,' she replied lightly. 'I wish them well, Leigh, though I don't think he's going to find life so easy, married to a TV star.'

'Frankly, I couldn't care less about them,' he said irritably. 'All that concerns me is how *you* must be feeling, Rose, and as long as you don't mind, Sykes can go to hell in his own way. Do you think he knew about her past — the son she seems to have left behind her?'

Rose turned and looked at him reproachfully.

'Poor Caroline! Fancy keeping quiet about that for all these years. And now she's discovered that nothing can be kept secret for ever.'

He realised that she was thinking about her mother, and clapped a hand to his mouth.

'Oh, Rose, what a blundering idiot I am! Forgive me, I didn't think.'

She squeezed his arm and smiled. 'It's all right, don't worry!' Then she drew away from him with a mischievous little chuckle.

'Come on, we shall be late for the booking clinic,'

she chided, and ran ahead of him, her slim legs and rounded hips presenting a very attractive back view.

Damn you, darling, he thought as he followed her into Outpatients.

Rose picked up her pen and prepared to interview the last patient of the session.

'Good afternoon, Mrs Bradshaw. Please take a seat. I believe the midwife has already seen you?' she smiled.

'Yes, Dr Gillis,' replied the patient, an attractive woman in her late thirties. A few grey hairs gleamed at her temples, and there were fine little lines around her eyes and mouth, etched by experience of life; nevertheless there was a radiant bloom on her face that had nothing to do with age and everything to do with happiness.

'Sister took my blood-pressure, weighed and measured me, tested my water and sent me to have blood samples taken,' she chuckled. 'Surely there can't be much else to be done!'

Rose glanced down at the case-notes and noted the midwife's observations. Everything seemed to be normal.

'No, not much,' she agreed. 'I just want to check on your medical and obstetric history, that's all.'

'That shouldn't take long, Doctor, seeing that I'm as fit as a fiddle, and this is my first pregnancy!'

'Ah, yés, I see,' said Rose, noting the word *primigravida*. 'How very nice to be having your first baby a little later in life.'

'Quite a bit later, Doctor. I'm nearly thirty-nine.'

Something in her voice made Rose look up and stare very hard at this delightful lady.

'Mrs Grace Bradshaw—have I seen you before

somewhere?' she asked as her memory began to ring a distant bell.

'You certainly have, Dr Rose.'

Rose tapped her forehead as she thought back.

'I'm sorry, but I just can't recall where we last met,' she apologised.

'I looked very different then,' smiled Mrs Bradshaw, 'covered in blood and dirt, my clothes were torn, and I was crying my eyes out because I thought my husband was going to die.'

And Rose remembered the M63 road accident, and the Bradshaws with their niece Peggy.

'Jesus, Mary and Joseph!' she exclaimed, rising to her feet and coming round the desk. She held out her arms, and the two women gave each other an ecstatic hug.

'Grace Bradshaw! And your husband Alfred — how is he?'

'Alive and kicking, and I'm here to prove it!' said Grace, laughing. 'Oh, Dr Gillis, I'm *pregnant*! I've come to book at your antenatal clinic!'

'But — you said you couldn't *have* any children,' gasped Rose.

'No, we *couldn't*! We'd been trying for years and years, and had given up all hope. Then when I'd missed two periods and noticed that my breasts were tingling and I had a bit of indigestion, I wondered what could be wrong — even my GP gave me some medicine for my stomach!'

'Never!' giggled Rose. 'He didn't!'

'He did! He's told me since that he didn't want to raise my hopes too soon, but I think he didn't twig — and then I began to be suspicious, and suspicion turned to hope, and then to certainty,' Grace confided, with tears of joy sparkling on her lashes. 'My GP says it must be due to the road accident. Something got shaken into the right position, probably a re-alignment of the ends of the Fallopian tubes. Apparently it's been known before that a tremendous shake-up has resulted in an unexpected pregnancy—oh, isn't it *wonderful*, Dr Gillis?'

'It most certainly *is*, Grace! Excuse me a moment, but I *must* call Dr McDowie in to see you,' insisted Rose, and a few minutes later Leigh came in, having heard that Rose wanted to have his opinion about the patient she was examining.

He recognised Grace at once, and stood staring at her almost nervously.

'Grace Bradshaw, by all that's holy,' he murmured. 'I daren't say anything—I made such a gaffe the last time we met. *You* must tell me what you're doing in an antenatal clinic.'

'I'm going to have a child, Doctor.'

He opened his arms and enfolded the expectant mother in a long, silent hug. Rose saw him close his eyes, and when at last he spoke, his voice was husky.

'My dear, there just couldn't be any better news than this.'

Rose went over to touch Grace's shoulder, whereupon Leigh freed one arm and pulled her towards him, enfolding both women in one embrace.

'Well, that's made our day!' he exclaimed, holding Grace at arm's length and looking her up and down in awestruck admiration. Going over to the desk, he wrote a very saucy message to Alfred on a prescription pad, tore it off and pressed it into Grace's hand.

'When's it due?' was the next question, and Grace revealed that she was just three months pregnant, the midwife having given her the provisional date of May the seventeenth.

'Just think about it, Rosie,' said Leigh at the end of the clinic session. 'There were two deaths as a result of that motorway pile-up—three, if you count Peggy Bradshaw's little foetus. And now there's a new life coming into the world because of it. Makes you think, eh?'

'I still can't believe it,' marvelled Rose. 'We'll have to take very special care of her, won't we?'

'You can say that again,' he agreed. 'I'll bet the old man does a Caesarean at thirty-eight weeks, just to make sure of an easy ride for the nipper.'

That evening Rose attended a mass in the hospital chapel, and to her surprise Leigh slipped in beside her. The gospel reading was St Luke's account of the angel's visit to the Virgin Mary, and for the two doctors there was a special meaning to the familiar words.

She felt his touch on her hand, and thought there was nowhere she would rather be than on duty in the maternity department when Christmas-time came this year.

But first there was the pantomime to be got through, and Rose had no wish to sit and watch the romantic scenes between the Sleeping Beauty and her Prince. On the night of the first performance, a Thursday, Rose spent her evening off visiting an old neighbour of her mother's who lived alone. When she returned to work the next day, the whole hospital was buzzing with success of the show.

'It was brilliant, Rose!' enthused David Rowan over coffee in the office. 'That charge nurse on ITU is a genius—he not only wrote the script, but played the part of the Royal Obstetrician, and looked the *image* of the old man, gold-rimmed half-moons, mannerisms and all! Eve and I were convulsed—and as for Leigh, he ought to have been a professional singer. He's so talented all round——'

He broke off as Leigh and Tanya came in.

'You weren't there last night, Rose!' Leigh said at once.

'Er—no, I had a previous engagement,' she apologised awkwardly. 'David says it was extremely good.'

'You'll be able to come tonight, won't you?' There was a certain personal interest in his look and tone.

'Actually I'm on call, so I don't really think I can make it,' she told him, feeling cowardly but unwilling to be pressured into an experience she felt certain would be painful.

'Oh, you *must* try to look in on *some* of it if you possibly can, Dr Gillis!' cried Tanya, delighted with the compliments she and Leigh were receiving.

'I'd appreciate it if you could, Rose,' said Leigh seriously in a low tone meant only for her, but David Rowan heard too, and smiled.

'I'm on call tonight, and I'll make sure to be around when the panto's on, Rose, so go and enjoy it with a clear conscience,' he assured her with misplaced generosity.

'Thanks, but I can't promise. We could be very busy this evening,' she said shortly, getting up and leaving the office. She walked briskly along the corridor towards the antenatal ward.

'Rose! Please, stop a minute, will you?'

She turned to find Leigh at her side. He had followed her, and now spoke with real insistence.

'I want you to be there, Rose. I have a special

reason. Take Rowan's offer, and make sure you get a front seat, there's a good girl!'

Rose's self-control, already stretched to breaking point, finally gave way.

'Oh, for God's sake, Leigh, what's it to you? What makes you think I'm so anxious to see you cavorting around in that ridiculous Sir Walter Raleigh outfit?' She knew she was being childish, but was so afraid of revealing her true feelings that she took refuge in anger.

'Rose, will you please *listen* to me? I've got something to say, and it won't wait much longer!' he said, raising his voice, and gripping her arm. Rose's nerves could stand no more.

'Leave me alone, damn you!' She shook off his arm, and as he recoiled, she burst out with: 'I don't *want* to listen to you! Go and tell it to your Sleeping Beauty instead—I think you'll find she's very much awake!'

Her voice broke on shameful tears, and she turned hastily aside from the door of the antenatal ward and made for the stairs, literally running away from him.

Leigh stood quite still as he watched her retreating back.

'Oh, my God,' he muttered to himself. 'I shall have to take a very drastic step to *make* you listen, Rose. Yes—I'll need some technical assistance, but I'll *do* it!'

As it happened, the delivery unit was indeed busy that evening, and there were several patients in labour; Rowan and Rose were kept well occupied, and when Rose saw Roger Maynard lurking in the corridor at one point, carrying some complicated equipment and a length of electrical wiring, she sped past him with only a quick nod. She knew that members of the pantomime cast were planning a visit to the wards after the show, and suspected that a lot of photographs would be taken. She made a mental note to stay well hidden in the delivery unit, out of the way of cameras.

She had just completed a forceps delivery in Delivery Room Two at ten o'clock. The pantomime would be ending now, she thought, and she was thankful to have a genuine excuse to stay hidden away. She sat down on the surgeon's stool to suture the episiotomy while Staff Nurse Laurie Moffatt attended to the baby, and had nearly finished when there was a crackling noise on the hospital broadcasting system which was normally relayed to the patients' earphones, but was now being picked up by a couple of amplifiers placed strategically on both floors of the maternity department.

To Rose's utter amazement the next thing they heard was Leigh's fine tenor voice singing 'True Love' at the close of the pantomime. The sound penetrated to every area of the department, even the delivery rooms. Rose's mouth tightened, and Laurie smiled knowingly.

'Isn't he *gorgeous*?' she sighed. 'Roger got it fixed up so that we could all hear him serenade us after the show!'

Rose tried to close her ears to this intrusion of sound. Her task completed, she and Laurie made the mother comfortable, then she began to write up the case-notes in the privacy of the delivery room.

And then she heard something she could not ignore. Leigh was speaking on the sound system, and his words made her heart miss a beat.

'And now, friends, I want to sing another song about love, dedicated to a very special lady doctor, and I mean every word of it. I hope you're listening, Rose —

if you're not, everybody else is. So with my heart in my mouth, here it is. Let Robbie Burns speak for me!'

There were a few introductory chords on the guitar, and then he began to sing the beautiful Scottish love-song. The words filled the air with such longing and sincerity that the patients and staff looked at each other, smiling and nodding. Rose stood where she was, entranced and unbelieving; was this miracle really happening?

'O, my Luve's like a red red rose
    That's newly sprung in June —— '

'Out you go, Dr Rose, and face the music!' ordered Laurie, and Rose was pushed firmly out of the delivery room and into the corridor; all over the department she was being searched for.

'Where's Dr Gillis?'

'Does she know he's singing this for her?'

'Look, there she is! Dr Rose! Dr Rose!'

And then she was surrounded by laughing faces, congratulating, teasing, kissing. She was the woman of the hour, eclipsing even the Sleeping Beauty, who now appeared in her splendid dress to visit the mothers in the antenatal ward. Rose hardly knew where to look as Tanya came straight up the corridor, her eyes bright and mouth firmly set. She was accompanied by the Royal Obstetrician who stayed close by her side.

'So it seems it was you all the time, Dr Gillis,' she said with a dignity that Rose could only admire. 'I hope you'll both be happy.'

'Thank you, Tanya, you look fabulous —— ' began Rose, but the Sleeping Beauty had swept away. From antenatal she hurried down to Postnatal with her admiring companion, where they were met with delighted applause.

Meanwhile the song continued to its haunting conclusion.

'And I will come again, my Luve,
    Tho' it were ten thousand mile.'

Rose now knew that she was loved by Leigh McDowie, and that he would soon confront her in Maternity. It was nearly half-past ten; pulling on her white coat, she ran down the stairs to the entrance through which he would come.

So when Prince Silversword in his Elizabethan costume opened the door, she was there to be gathered into his outstretched arms. He threw off his feathered cap, and held her close against the blue velvet tunic.

'Darling Rose, I'm sorry to be all ponced up like this ——'

'I wouldn't care if you were dressed as the Wicked Witch!' she laughed in sheer joy. 'Oh, Leigh, that song! That wonderful song!'

'And did you *listen* to it, my love?' he asked gently. 'Did you listen and believe it?'

'Yes, oh, yes! And you really love me, Leigh, knowing all you do?'

The depth and sweetness of his long kiss on her eager lips was answer enough, and he was assured that his love was abundantly returned.

She disengaged herself at last.

'I must go back to the unit, Your Royal Highness,' she whispered.

'Yes, and I suppose I must pay my visit to the mamas and the babas before they kip down for the night,' he said with a chuckle. 'Any later, and they'll think I'm the ghost of Sir Walter Raleigh, and scream the place

down. But listen, Rose, I want to marry you—Brigid
wouldn't have wanted us to hang about, she had her
eye on me for you from the start! Look, I can arrange
for a locum SHO to come in on Sunday to cover for us.
Will you come up to Carlisle with me and meet my
parents?'

She covered her heart with her hand. 'This Sunday?
The day after tomorrow? Oh, no, Leigh, it's *much* too
short notice!' she cried in dismay.

'Good, that's settled! I'll give them a ring tomorrow,
and tell them we'll be there for dinner on Sunday!' he
said with satisfaction. 'It's only just over a hundred
miles up the M6, we can do it in an hour and a half.
Don't worry, my darling, they'll love you—Andrew
already does!'

He kissed her again, checking her protests, and then
with a last loving look they parted at the foot of the
stairs.

The McDowies' welcome to Rose was warm and sympathetic. His Scottish lawyer father told her they were
relieved to know that Leigh was ready to settle down,
and his Yorkshire-born mother was obviously pleased
with his choice. Nevertheless, Rose was painfully shy
at first, and felt she could hardly eat the excellent
dinner. Mrs McDowie had even boiled the Christmas
pudding she had made the previous month.

'You won't be here for Christmas, so we might as
well celebrate it now,' she said pleasantly.

The wedding was to take place when Leigh and Rose
finished their housemanship in mid-January. Because
of Rose's recent bereavement, and the fact that they
belonged to different churches, a quiet wedding in the
hospital chapel was planned. It was also decided that

they would live in Rose's home until they knew where they would eventually settle. Leigh had applied for a partnership in a group practice in Chorlton, and wanted Rose to consider becoming a GP as well.

'But you'll both be called Dr McDowie, and people won't know which one they want!' joked his father.

'I know which one *I'd* want!' quipped Andrew, and Rose felt grateful for his cheeky but friendly presence.

'Are you sure he's right for you, Rose?' he asked with a grave face. 'He's been very slow at courting, considering that he was besotted with you when you came to *The Tempest*!'

'That was quite by chance — Leigh was given a couple of free tickets by a patient,' said Rose innocently.

'Really? If you believed *that*, Rose, you'd believe anything!' grinned Andrew. 'I bet he bought those tickets with you in mind!'

Rose glanced at Leigh and saw reluctant confirmation of his brother's guess. She blushed furiously, not realising how much this endeared her to her future in-laws.

Driving back to Manchester in the early dusk, Rose felt wrapped in a little cocoon of happiness, seated beside her fiancé and knowing that she had acquitted herself well. She was overwhelmingly relieved by the success of the day, with a promise of a deepening relationship as she came to know the McDowies better. Leigh sensed her relaxed mood, in contrast to the tension of the outward journey, and he drew her head on to his shoulder.

'You made a big hit with them, my darling, and I'm proud of you.'

'I think they were a little taken aback to hear how

soon we're getting married,' she said shyly. 'I wonder if they think we're — er — in a hurry.'

'I *am* in a hurry!' he assured her with a grin.

She snuggled close against him, and gave way to the drowsiness which overcame her after the strains of the day; she fell into a blissful doze, her face buried against his jacket.

'Wake up, darling, we're here,' she heard him say, and realised that they had reached the little terraced house in Beltonshaw. It was all in darkness.

'Goodness, how quickly we've got here!' she exclaimed, undoing her seatbelt. When Leigh did not move, she turned to him with a question in her soft dark blue eyes.

'You're coming in, of course, Leigh?'

'Am I invited, Rose?'

She knew exactly what he meant. If he came into her home, it would not just be for coffee and a goodnight kiss. Neither of them were due back at the hospital until eight the next morning. The choice was hers, and she did not hesitate.

'Of course you are! Come *home*, Leigh,' she said simply, and he needed no persuasion.

Once indoors, she switched on the lights and lit the gas fire.

'Take a seat, and I'll make some coffee,' she said, removing her coat and throwing it over a chair. She went out into the kitchen, and he sat down on the settee.

'Anything on TV tonight?' she called out. 'There's the *Radio Times* on the table.'

He did not reply, and as she poured boiling water into two mugs with instant coffee, she wondered if he would prefer some music.

'There are some tapes in the cabinet beside you, Leigh, if you'd care to look through them.'

She heard the opening bars of Vivaldi's *The Four Seasons*, and realised he had anticipated her.

'Oh, lovely! One of my favourites,' she smiled as she came in with a small tray and sat down beside him, talking with rather formal politeness because she was suddenly overcome with shyness.

'Would you like a poached egg or something on toast?' she asked brightly.

'Rose.'

Just the one word, but she trembled as his right arm encircled her and his left hand touched the side of her face, gently but firmly turning her head towards him.

'"*So deep in luve am I*",' he quoted, and as her arms went round his neck he began to kiss her, softly and invitingly, so that she responded slowly, then deepening into an explorative urgency that made her heart pound. She gasped and gave a little incredulous cry as his hand stole under her blouse, lifting it up, finding her bra and unhooking the back fastening. She drew a sharp breath of sheer pleasure at the touch of his lips on her breasts, first one rosy tip and then the other. Then he became more demanding, drawing the tender flesh into his mouth while he stroked her bared waist, her back, her body beneath the unfastened skirt. His hands had all the bold possessiveness of a lover—a master.

Beside the glowing fire, their clothes seemed to melt away in a randomly discarded scatter on the settee and floor. She gazed at his dark eyes as they searched hers, a lock of hair falling over his forehead—that unprofessionally long hair! He looked about twenty-five, a young man about to claim his first love.

'I can't wait any longer, Rose — I've wanted you for such a long, long time ——'

He was as breathless as herself, and trembled as they eagerly discovered each other's nakedness, the joy of revelation that occurred when a loving friendship between a man and a woman embarked upon the new dimension of physical intimacy. Rose sighed with wonder as she saw and touched the proof of his passion for her, and they both uttered a low cry when he entered the moist warmth of her secret place that was so ready to receive him; within only a few seconds they both reached a climax in which for a timeless moment they were suspended between heaven and earth, a voyage among the stars of the winter night.

Slowly descending again to the strains of Vivaldi's lovely music, Rose found herself being cradled and caressed in Leigh's arms as he told her over and over again how much he loved her.

'We have to be married as soon as possible, dearest Rose,' he said seriously. 'It must be before the year's out! I'll see the Registrar tomorrow about getting a special licence, and you must have a word with Father Naylor. We have to make this legal, my darling.'

Rose could only respond with a loving look and a kiss for this man who was so anxious to marry her after possessing her.

The music came to an end, and when Rose gave a little shiver, Leigh got up and helped her to her feet.

'Come to bed, my love.'


The marriage took place in the hospital chapel on New Year's Eve at midday, so that Andrew could attend before going on stage in the evening. The day was bright but cold, and Rose wore a light grey wool suit with a soft dove-coloured velvet hat trimmed with a single large red rose. She carried a prayer-book as she walked slowly up the short aisle on the arm of her friend Derek Horsfield while the organ played a Handel voluntary. The little chapel was still decorated with holly and ivy after the Christmas services, and tall candles glowed with a warm brightness that reflected the joy of the occasion. The many friends and colleagues of the bride and groom filled the seats, and the McDowie family occupied the front row, together with Miss Maura Carlinnagh, who had flown over from County Clare to see her niece married. Thoughts of her sister Brigid inevitably came to Maura's mind, but she was greatly comforted by the knowledge that Brigid's prayers had been answered, and Rose was marrying the right doctor, 'that lovely doctor. . .wid a look in his eye'.

David and Eve Rowan were early arrivals, and whispered to Fay Grant and Susannah Okoje that their sadness over Eve's miscarriage had given way to relief at having achieved nearly ten weeks of a second pregnancy. Philip and Annette Cranstone found a seat beside Paul Sykes, whose fiancée was unable to attend as she was rehearsing for a new TV series. The midwives had turned out in force to see their champion married to the gorgeous Leigh McDowie, and even Tanya Dickenson had put on a brave face and arrived with a uniformed Sister Pardoe, Angela Grierson and Laurie Moffatt.

But the big surprise was the number of ex-patients who turned up at the doctors' wedding. Dorothy Beddows came in with Philippa and baby Bella; Mr and Mrs Mowbray proudly carried their bonny six-month-old son, next to Mrs Lambert and her baby girl.

A pale but smiling Trish Pendle came in with a yelling baby Donovan, and a very special expectant couple occupied a seat at the back: Grace and Alfred Bradshaw, now just halfway through their wait for their precious baby.

Rose was aware of all the loving thoughts that surrounded her as she looked up at the man who stood waiting for her with the priest at the altar. She saw the smiles of his parents and Andrew the best man who were so happy to welcome her into the McDowie clan.

She inclined her head towards Mr Horsfield, who bowed slightly and stepped back as they reached the altar rail; Leigh held out his hand to her and drew her to his side, to face Father Naylor. Everybody in the chapel heard their firm, clear responses as the vows were exchanged, and when the ceremony was over they turned to face the congregation.

Together they stood on the threshold of a New Year and a new life. Leigh was about to embark on a new chapter in his profession, but Rose looked a little thoughtful, because, being a woman, she knew that there would soon be an interruption to her own career as a doctor.

She clasped her husband's hand and faced the future with joyful confidence, serene in the knowledge of his love; and everybody agreed that she was the most radiant of brides.

# EXPERIENCE THE EXOTIC

# 4 MEDICAL ROMANCES
# AND 2 FREE GIFTS
## FROM MILLS & BOON

Capture all the drama and emotion of a hectic medical world when you accept 4 Medical Romances PLUS a cuddly teddy bear and a mystery gift - absolutely FREE and without obligation. And, if you choose, go on to enjoy 4 exciting Medical Romances every month for only £1.70 each! Be sure to return the coupon below today to: **Mills & Boon Reader Service, FREEPOST, PO Box 236, Croydon, Surrey CR9 9EL.**

◄ — — — — — ┤ **NO STAMP REQUIRED** ├ — — — —

**YES!** Please rush me 4 FREE Medical Romances and 2 FREE gifts! Please also reserve me a Reader Service subscription, which means I can look forward to receiving 4 brand new Medical Romances for only £6.80 every month, postage and packing FREE. If I choose not to subscribe, I shall write to you within 10 days and still keep my FREE books and gifts. I may cancel or suspend my subscription at any time. I am over 18 years.
Please write in BLOCK CAPITALS.

Ms/Mrs/Miss/Mr _____ **EP53D**

Address _____

_____

_____

Postcode _____ Signature _____

**mps**
MAILING
PREFERENCE
SERVICE

## — *MEDICAL* /*ROMANCE* —

The books for enjoyment this month are:

**A BORDER PRACTICE** Drusilla Douglas
**A SONG FOR DR ROSE** Margaret Holt
**THE LAST EDEN** Marion Lennox
**HANDFUL OF DREAMS** Margaret O'Neill

❤    ❤    ❤    ❤    ❤

### Treats in store!

Watch next month for the following absorbing stories:

**JUST WHAT THE DOCTOR ORDERED** Caroline Anderson
**LABOUR OF LOVE** Janet Ferguson
**THE FAITHFUL TYPE** Elizabeth Harrison
**A CERTAIN HUNGER** Stella Whitelaw